I0612155

# THE SUMMONED HERO

SUMMONED TO ANOTHER WORD AND FORCE TO
FIGHT THE DEMON KING

BOOK ONE

## JAMES E. WISHER

SAND HILL PUBLISHING

Copyright © 2025 by James Wisher

All rights reserved.

No part of this book may be reproduced in any form or by any electronic or mechanical means, including information storage and retrieval systems, without written permission from the author, except for the use of brief quotations in a book review.

Edited by: Janie Linn Dullard

Cover art by: B-Ro

030620251.0

# CHAPTER 1

Danny took a deep breath of salty sea air as the ocean breeze blew past. It held a hint of rot today. From the direction, he figured it must be blowing over the base's dump. He and his team had only been transferred to Marine Base Six a week ago. Situated on a peninsula jutting into the Pacific Ocean on the southernmost island in the Empire of the Rising Sun's main chain, Base Six was primarily a recovery base. Soldiers wounded in action around the world were sent here for however long it took to get them combat ready again.

He touched his stomach where the shrapnel had struck. The scar still itched three months later though thankfully it no longer hurt. The doc said it was pure luck that the metal hit where it did. A few inches higher and Danny would've bled out on the battlefield the same as two of his less fortunate teammates.

Damn terrorists. Their IED had knocked the team for a loop. They were lucky it was a set-and-forget model and none of the enemy was nearby to finish off the wounded.

JAMES E. WISHER

That was the only thing lucky about the situation. Nothing good ever happened when you were playing in the sandbox. If you weren't getting shot at, you were getting blown up. The food sucked and the living quarters at Firebase Three sucked harder. The glamorous life of a Marine was everything his father warned him about when he tried to talk Danny out of joining.

He blew out a breath and turned to look out over the ocean. It was peaceful here, despite being only a couple hundred miles from the Iron Empire. Maybe that was why they didn't bring soldiers straight home to the Alliance for their recovery. Danny had no clue himself. Someone far further up the chain than a mere lance corporal had no doubt decided it was a good idea and if a general decided that, then everyone of lower rank would agree.

The growl of an approaching Jeep preceded a familiar voice shouting, "Yo, DJ! You coming with us or not?"

Private first class Eric Young stood in the back of an overloaded Jeep, his uniform unbuttoned to show off an impressive physique. It also showed off the two bullet wounds Eric had picked up on their last deployment. The rest of the squad was jammed into the front and back, practically sitting on each other's laps.

"I told you, Suzy'd kill me if she found out I visited the geishas."

"Man, she's half a world away in Sentinel City. How's she ever going to find out?"

"She'll take one look at my guilty face and know I screwed up somehow and when she asks me, I'll have to tell her. We swore never to lie to each other. So you boys have fun and make damn sure you're back on base when that eight-hour pass runs out."

"So you just gonna waste our first pass in a month hanging out here?" Eric asked.

Danny shook his head. "No, I'm going to take a walk through the shopping district. See if I can get a good deal on a ring."

"Finally work up the guts to pop the question?" Hunter asked.

Danny grinned. "I've got six months left on my enlistment. Suzy graduates from college two months after that. Soon as she gets her diploma, I'll be on one knee with my fingers crossed."

Eric laughed. "Man, you're too young to be getting married. You should party hard until thirty at least, then settle down. You're fucking it all up."

Danny shook his head. "Get out of here. And remember to behave yourselves. This is an allied nation and we're guests. Your actions reflect on the Marines and the Alliance."

"You're such a stiff," Eric said, still laughing. "Hit it, Hopkins. We're out of here."

The Jeep sped away and Danny followed it toward the gate at a more sedate pace. They were all good guys. At twenty-two, Danny only had three or four years on them, but sometimes he felt way older. Three years of dodging bullets in the desert aged you in a hurry. It also made you appreciate the important things in life.

The MP on duty at the front gate took a cursory look at Danny's pass and waved him through. The shopping district was only a mile from base and it was a beautiful morning for a walk.

Danny ambled along the sidewalk, pausing only to wave at the driver of a deuce and a half bringing in supplies. The big trucks came and went at all hours of the day and night, their diesel engines filling the crisp air with sulfur.

He'd worked with the quartermaster for a month between deployments and found he had a knack for organization. His hope was to find a job with a logistics company when he left the Marines.

A little smile creased his lips. When he left, not if. Whenever his CO asked if he planned to reenlist, Danny would hem and haw without giving a real answer. But in his heart he knew when his time was up, he was done. He already had nightmares about the men he'd killed. Adding more faces to the collection didn't appeal to him at all. Getting shot or blown up again appealed to him even less. He'd avoided the Reaper so far; no sense pushing his luck.

The shopping district consisted of walking paths lined with shops and stands. The smell of sizzling meat filled the air despite lunch being a few hours away. A modest crowd browsed the offerings, mostly locals, but he spotted a couple of tan uniforms mixed in. You could buy pretty much anything on this street, including jewelry.

He passed clothing stores, a noodle shop, and a guy selling no doubt dubiously sourced CDs out of the trunk of his trike. Finally, he reached the jewelry store and stepped inside.

Glass cases filled with jewelry ran along both walls as well as a few that were scattered in the middle. Danny went right to the rings. Lance corporals didn't make enough to let him buy Suzy the ring she deserved, but he'd try to find something she'd like.

"Can I help you, young man?" A woman old enough to be his grandmother came hobbling up.

"I'm looking for a diamond ring. Something pretty that a girl would like."

Her face crinkled as she smiled. "You're a bit young, but I guess when you're in love, you're in love."

She opened the case and after a moment brought out a thin gold ring with a diamond that looked way too big to be either real or in his price range. "I'm not sure…"

"I'll give you a good price, dear. A lady likes a little sparkle when she gets a ring. Do you like the design?"

Danny nodded. More importantly, he thought Suzy would love it. "How much?"

She quoted a price that was only three-quarters of what he'd saved up. It seemed too good to be true.

"Are you sure? Figured I'd have to spend way more."

"I'm old. There's more than enough money in my bank account but not nearly enough love in the world. Consider this deal my tiny contribution to correcting the imbalance."

Danny would've hugged her, but Imperials tended to dislike being touched. Instead he offered his brightest smile. "In that case I'd be happy to buy the ring. Thank you very much."

A swipe of his debit card and a signature later and Danny had his engagement ring. It was absolutely perfect. He couldn't wait to see the look on Suzy's face when he showed it to her. It was going to be a long eight months, but so worth the wait.

He pocketed the little box and stepped back into the street, his stride lighter than air when he turned toward the base. There was a beach nearby. He'd take a long walk then head to the mess hall for lunch.

Three steps later the worst pain Danny had ever experienced wracked his whole body. He collapsed and stared up at the sky. A white tunnel appeared above him. It felt like something was sucking the life out of him. Was this the white light people talked about when you died?

Danny fought with everything he had to resist. He couldn't die now. Not when he had so much to live for.

Struggle as he might, the pain only grew worse until, with a final wrench, he was flying through the sky. He looked back and saw his unmoving body lying on the ground surrounded by anxious figures.

His last thought was that he hoped no one stole Suzy's ring.

# CHAPTER 2

Vague, muddled voices woke Danny from a deep sleep. He was lying on something hard and smooth. That's when it all came back to him. The shop, the ring, the pain, and finally the vortex of white light. He'd assumed he was dying, but he didn't feel dead.

He tried to open his eyes, but his eyelids didn't want to cooperate. His right arm was similarly unwilling to obey his will. Maybe he had a stroke and ended up paralyzed. The thought petrified him for the few seconds it took to remember that the military employed light magic healers exactly for this type of thing. Even if he was paralyzed, they'd have someone fix him up soon. Soon, of course, being a relative term when talking about the military.

As he lay on the hard surface, unable to move, the voices slowly started to make sense. Sounded like two women, probably nurses. No, that didn't make sense. If he was in the hospital he'd be lying in a bed, not on the ground. EMTs maybe.

He stilled his mind and tried to focus.

"I don't know why he hasn't woken up." That sounded more like a girl than a grown woman. Maybe even a teenager. "The summoning spell worked perfectly and his soul has been fused with his new host. There was considerable resistance. That may be delaying his awakening."

"Have you tried a healing spell?" An older sounding voice. She reminded Danny of his mother.

"Yes, but nothing happened. There's no injury to heal. It may just take longer than the text describes. The ritual has only been activated six times previously. That's not a lot of information to go on."

"His Majesty is growing anxious. Perhaps if we splash him with cold water."

Danny had no desire to get splashed with cold water. He fought with all his might to open his eyes and finally they obliged. Brilliant white light dazzled him. It looked like a ceiling made of diamonds far above his head.

He blinked a few times and the blurriness cleared up. The ceiling still looked like diamonds. Definitely not a hospital room then. Having been shot and blown up, Danny was all too familiar with them.

Taking a deep breath, he mustered all his focus. "Hello?"

The word came out jumbled and nearly incomprehensible, but he did make a sound at least. That brought two sets of footsteps. Two women, he assumed the ones he'd heard speaking a moment ago, appeared in his field of view.

The one on his right looked to be in her midteens, with long, beautiful blond hair, a pale, angelic face, and bright-blue eyes. She wore a white robe emblazoned with gold markings he couldn't read.

On his left stood an older woman in a similar robe, maybe in her midthirties, with equally blond hair cut shoulder length, and a far less angelic appearance. She gave the same vibe as a teacher who suspected one of her students was pretending to be sick to avoid a test.

"Are you okay, Hero?" the younger woman asked.

Hero? What the hell was she talking about? Danny was no hero, just a regular soldier.

"Where am I?" The words came out less garbled this time. That had to be a good sign.

The girl smiled. "This is the Crystal Cathedral, a temple dedicated to Adonael, archangel of justice and nobility."

The name meant nothing to Danny. The only archangel he knew was the Goddess, Lady of Healing. As soon as the thought formed, knowledge of Adonael flooded into him. She was the patron of the Kingdom of Villipan and savior of Valindor. Valindor being the name of this planet. How Danny knew that he couldn't say, but the certainty that he was no longer on Earth shook him to the core.

It must have shown on his face because the older woman said, "The host body's knowledge is starting to fuse with the knowledge retained by his soul. There will be some confusion until the process is complete."

"Agreed," the younger one said. "And if his psyches are still separate, his body has hours before it's functional. Perhaps you should tell His Majesty that an introduction will have to wait until this evening."

Judging by the way her face twisted up, Danny suspected the older woman would prefer to do just about anything else. As in the military, no one liked having to tell their superior a problem had popped up.

"I suppose that would be best. I'll leave you to it." The older woman moved out of his view and her footsteps quickly receded.

"What's your name?" Danny asked. The words were coming easier now, but he knew they weren't English words. Probably best not to think too hard about what that meant.

"Ah, forgive my rudeness, Hero. I'm Eve Carre, chosen priestess of Adonael. It's a great honor to meet you."

He tried to sit up, but got nothing for his effort. At least his mind was clear. "Daniel J. Smith. The last thing I remember is collapsing in the shopping district and getting sucked into a white tunnel. I assumed I was dying, but now I'm not so sure."

"What you saw was the ethereal tunnel connecting our worlds. The magic pulled your soul out of your body, brought it across the vastness of space, and fused it with your new host. Full integration takes time. That's why you can't move yet. Your mental faculties seem fully restored. That's an excellent sign. Have you begun to access the host's knowledge yet?"

Danny wasn't sure what to make of that first part so he focused on her question for now. "I know you're not speaking English, yet I can understand you perfectly. I know this place is called Villipan on the world of Valindor. It's like there's more, but it feels like having a library in my mind rather than knowledge I learned myself."

"That's another function of the incomplete integration. You'll continue to get bursts of knowledge as you experience new things. It will be overwhelming at first. Take your time and don't worry. Everyone is here to help you, Hero."

"Daniel. You called me Hero before. Why?"

"Because you're the one that's been brought to our world

to fight the demon king and save us all. That's the hero's job. I had the honor of being chosen to oversee the ritual that transported you here. It can only be performed once every hundred years and only when the new demon king has been confirmed. That unfortunate event happened three days ago."

This was all insane. He didn't know whether to feel rage at being dragged here against his will, flattered that these people thought he was capable of saving them, or something else altogether.

He wanted to rub his forehead and to his surprise his right hand lifted about six inches off the table.

Since he seemed incapable of doing anything else Danny asked, "Assuming I can do what you want, you can send me back, can't you?"

Eve slumped, her bright smile fading. "Unfortunately, no. Physical bodies can't pass between worlds, not with the magic we have anyway. The elves managed it, but their master mages are long gone. Our technique is a pale imitation of what they used. We only brought your soul here. Your original body is, I'm afraid, very dead. And with no body to return you to, even if we had the ability, we couldn't send you back."

Now Danny's anger flared. Hot and bright, it rushed through him like liquid fire. He sat up and wrapped his right hand around the girl's neck. "Who are you to play The Creator with my life? I had plans, friends, family, a woman I loved, and you've taken it all."

When she didn't respond he gave her a shake. "Answer me!"

Eve's mouth opened and closed as her face got redder and redder.

Right, she couldn't answer if he strangled her. Danny let her go and as soon as he did the fire vanished and he slumped back on the table.

Eve coughed, then ran a glowing hand along her neck. The dark finger marks Danny left on her throat vanished.

"I understand you're upset. And we wouldn't have brought you here had our situation not been so desperate. The truth is, the spell doesn't target anyone in particular. It targets a person, in a place called the Empire of the Rising Sun, with the greatest magical potential. You had the ill luck to fulfill the spell's requirements."

Danny let out a bitter laugh. These idiots summoned the wrong person. "Only one man on my world can use magic, and it certainly isn't me."

"You misunderstand. The magic of this world and the magic of yours is different. You might not be able to use magic on your world, but here, you're the most powerful magic user around. Or you will be once you're properly trained. You already used it once. Didn't you feel the ether surge through your body when you attacked me?"

Danny frowned. He'd certainly felt something. What, exactly, he was less certain. "So let me get this straight. You ripped my soul out of my body, killing it in the process. You then dragged my soul to your world and stuck it in some other poor sucker I assume you killed before I got here. And your plan is to teach me to use magic so I can kill some guy I don't know and who has never ripped my soul out of my body or done me any other harm. When I say it out loud, does it sound as crazy to you as it does to me?"

"It certainly is an extraordinary situation," Eve agreed. "But you're wrong about a couple of things. First, we didn't kill your host body. The young man volunteered to be your host. He trained and studied hard, winning a competition for the honor. All the knowledge and skills he attained during his life now belong to you. They just need to be drawn out."

"Wait, you're telling me some guy volunteered to die so I could use his body? You're joking."

"No, I assure you I'm quite serious. The ritual won't work if the host isn't willing. His self-sacrifice is the trigger. In sorcery, there's nothing more powerful than a soul freely given. Everyone here knows the danger the demon king represents. They also know the hero is our only hope of victory. Giving up his life in the hope that the rest of his family will be saved was a very noble thing."

Sacrificing himself to save his family. Kind of like a soldier jumping on a grenade to protect his comrades. Danny understood the sentiment. Not that it made what they did to him any more palatable.

"Okay, what else did I get wrong?"

"You said the demon king hasn't done you any harm, and he hasn't, yet. But this is your world now, whether you wish it or not. And assuming you don't want to live as a demon's slave, you'll have to fight."

"That's handy for you, isn't it?"

Danny clenched and relaxed his hands. There was certainly something to what she said, but he didn't have to like it. For now he'd play along, learn everything he could, and make his own decision when the time came.

He sat up again, this time without using magic. Everything seemed to be working a little better. "I'm going to try and walk around a bit. Do you have a cane or something? I'm still not feeling very steady."

Eve hurried to stand beside him. "I'll support you. That's what Adonael chose me for after all."

The way she said it made him think she meant it in more ways than just helping him walk. He had to give her credit. He'd almost broken her neck, yet she hadn't fled or acted as if he scared her. She was either very brave or very dumb.

Either way, he was starting to like her.

# CHAPTER 3

D anny walked—no, that was overly generous—he hobbled around the Crystal Cathedral, leaning heavily on Eve as he went. He'd seen Marines in rehab learning to walk again after having their spine severed and reattached with magic. They were more agile than Danny. He felt like a newborn fawn taking its first steps.

He glanced around at the empty hall. Three sections of fifty rows of pews each faced the altar where Danny woke up. He guessed this place held a thousand people at a time minimum. He'd seen a few churches dedicated to the Goddess back home, but most people he knew didn't worry much about religion. As long as you didn't draw the Reaper's attention, that was good enough.

Rumors were circulating that things were changing in the spiritual world, but he paid little enough attention to them. Staying alive and doing his job had been enough to worry about.

"You're doing really well," Eve said, jarring him out of his thoughts.

"Thanks. My legs are feeling better already. Are you sure I'm not too heavy?"

"No, I'm fine. Thank you for asking. Body strengthening magic makes it easy to support your weight."

Right, she was a priestess. "You said Adonael chose you to summon and support me. What, exactly, does that mean?"

"It means that I will help you in any way I can. When you're injured, I'll heal you. If you have questions, I'll answer them to the best of my ability. Whatever you need, if it's within my power to give it to you, I will. Lady Shael will oversee your combat training. I'm useless for that sort of thing, and when the final battle comes, you'll have to face the demon king alone. But other than that, I'm here for you."

Feeling a little better, Danny shifted more of his weight to his legs. They didn't buckle, which he took as a promising sign.

"Who's Lady Shael?"

"She's an elf-blood warrior mage of great skill. Her official title is Champion of Villipan and Trainer of Heroes. She trained each of the six previous heroes, making them strong enough to defeat their generation's demon king. I'm sure she'll do the same for you."

Danny grunted. Whenever he thought of elves, all that came to mind were his grandfather's stories about the war. According to family lore, twelve of Danny's ancestors had died fighting the elves. Despite all the time that had passed, that wasn't something anyone would forget. And his family wasn't the only one to suffer great losses. A lot of humans died when those bastards invaded. Even though humanity had won, the price had been high.

After five laps around the cathedral, Danny took his arm

off of Eve's shoulders and straightened. He wasn't ready to run an obstacle course, but he could walk on his own now.

He looked up from his now-much-steadier feet and caught a glimpse of his reflection in a polished crystal. Danny stopped dead in his tracks. His skin was pale, and his hair, long and blond, was tied back in a ponytail. Sparkling blue eyes stared back at him. He was dressed like he planned to attend one of the renaissance festivals his brother enjoyed so much: in a green tunic and tan trousers.

Some small part of him hadn't wanted to believe he really was in a new body, but it was impossible to deny now. He looked nothing like the man he'd been. Not that he looked bad, just totally different.

"Is everything okay?" Eve asked.

"Yeah, fine. I guess I didn't realize how different this new body was from my old one. It surprised me, that's all." In fact, the more he looked, the more he realized he resembled Eve. "Are you related to this body?"

"No. You'll find that the vast majority of people in Villipan look like we do, especially among the nobility. Darker hair does happen and some are less pale, but other than that, we all pretty much look like this."

That made sense. Assuming this world lacked mass transit, different ethnic groups wouldn't mingle much. Well, whatever. He had far more important things to worry about than demographics.

"If you're feeling up to it, we shouldn't keep His Majesty waiting any longer than necessary."

"I'm as ready to meet a king as I'm liable to be. Show me the way."

Eve smiled. "Don't be nervous. You're the savior of this

world. Everyone is on your side. Don't forget, if anything happens to you, we're all doomed."

Danny grinned. "So no pressure."

She stared at him in obvious confusion. "Excuse me?"

"Nothing. Let's go." Looked like that wasn't an expression they used here. No doubt one of many verbal mistakes Danny would make.

Eve led the way out the Crystal Cathedral's front door, down a set of steps, and onto the cobblestone street that went straight ahead as far as he could see. Side streets branched off to the left and right. Two-story buildings he assumed were businesses lined both sides. Danny glanced right, where a massive castle towered over the surrounding buildings. Red pennants fluttered from the top of the many towers. To the left were yet more of the small wood-and-stone structures. It was the very image of a fantasy city. His little brother would've flipped if he saw something like this.

One thing that was missing was the people.

"Where is everyone?"

"It's midday, so likely working. This is a mainly residential district for wealthy merchants and minor nobles. The higher-ranking nobles live on estates outside the city limits."

Images flashed through Danny's head: an older, severe-looking man and a kind woman. Three boys older than him and a younger girl. Parents and siblings along with a modest estate in the country. He massaged his temples, trying to will the unwelcome thoughts away.

"Daniel, are you okay?"

Danny realized he'd stopped dead in the middle of the street. "Sorry. Some memories of my host popped up. They took me by surprise. There were no names or emotions attached to them, but I saw a father, mother, three brothers, and a sister. I imagine they're all upset that their relative is dead."

"A little, I'm sure, but it's a great honor to serve as the host of the hero's soul. And that honor will extend to his family as well. Their sacrifice will be rewarded."

"That's good I guess." All Danny's parents would get, if they were lucky, was whatever tiny retirement Danny had built up during his time in the Marines.

They set out again and Eve turned down the first street to the right. They passed a few more-elaborate houses as well as a market that smelled of smoked sausages. Danny's mouth watered, but he kept quiet. If his nervousness got the best of him it wouldn't be wise to have a full stomach lest he vomit on the king's no-doubt-expensive shoes.

The street led right to the wall surrounding the castle Danny spotted earlier, passing through an arched gateway guarded by ten soldiers. They were dressed in armor with lions on the chest and carried some kind of spear with an ax head on one side.

As soon as they saw Eve they scrambled to attention and bowed. One of the men, the one in charge Danny assumed, said, "Welcome, Priestess. Is he..?"

"This generation's hero, yes. I've brought him to meet with the king. Would you send a runner to the castle to let them know we've arrived?"

The guard was staring at Danny in a way that made him rather uncomfortable. Luckily he snapped out of it and said, "Of course."

A different guard leaned his spear against the wall and sprinted toward the castle at an impressive clip considering how much armor he was wearing.

"An honor to meet you, Hero," the head guard said.

Danny held out his hand. "Daniel, nice to meet you too."

After a moment's hesitation they shook and the guard grinned like someone that met their favorite movie star. It probably wasn't that different for these people. Just because Danny didn't feel like a hero didn't mean they didn't see him as one.

"Let's keep going," Eve said. "They'll be expecting us."

Danny followed Eve through the gate, passing under a spiked portcullis and into a dirt yard. It was about forty yards from the gate to the huge wooden front door of the castle. That was open as well and a fancily dressed man holding an equally fancy walking stick was waiting for them.

"Who's that?" Danny asked.

"Jean-Michael Beouman, His Majesty's majordomo. He'll walk us to the throne room. Once we arrive, the herald will announce us, the door will open, and we'll walk to the throne. We bow to the royal family and then wait for the king to speak first. Answer his questions and be polite. You're a hero, not a courtier; no one expects perfect manners from you. Respect is sufficient."

They reached the front door and Jean bowed to them. Now that they were closer Danny took a better look at him. Other than a gaudy red robe embroidered with gold lions, he wasn't especially remarkable. Middling height and build, no visible weapon aside from the fancy walking stick. Danny had seen plenty of more intimidating people in his life.

"Welcome, Priestess. Welcome, Hero. Castle de Villipan is honored by your visit. Allow me to escort you to where His Majesty is waiting."

"Thank you, Jean. We humbly accept your welcome and offer our apologies for keeping His Majesty waiting." Eve offered a bow—a shallow one Danny noted—of her own.

The niceties taken care of, Jean turned and said, "This way, please."

They followed him down a red-carpeted hall decorated with paintings of regal men and beautiful women, all of them blond, pale and looking like they might have been Danny's relatives. A right turn brought another hall, this one lined with suits of armor. At the end of it was a closed door guarded by two people in armor just like the ones on display and each holding a spear like the guards outside.

Five feet from the door Jean said, "Wait here, please."

They stopped and Jean continued on alone, no doubt going to talk with the herald. The guards ignored him as he stuck his head inside the door.

"Is there going to be a crowd? I'm not great with large groups."

"No, this is an introduction strictly for the royal family and Lady Shael. At some point there will be a formal introduction where you'll meet most of the higher-ranking nobles, but not on the day you were summoned."

Thank heaven for small favors. Though if he was just meeting the royal family, all this fuss struck him as excessive.

After a minute the door opened and a thunderous voice said, "High Priestess Eve Carre and the Hero!"

When he didn't move, Eve grabbed his cuff and dragged him forward. They strode through the door. Another red carpet led to a slightly raised dais where a smooth-shaved blond man sat on a throne decorated with gold lions. He wore crimson robes and a simple gold circlet. Cold, ice-blue eyes stared holes into Danny.

Trying his best to ignore the intense stare, Danny shifted his gaze to the middle-aged woman seated beside him in a somewhat less fancy chair. She wore a matching crimson dress decorated with, no surprise, golden lions.

This had to be the king and queen. Behind them stood two young women and a young man dressed in similar outfits. A prince and two princesses. The girls were knock-outs, like supermodel hot. The prince had a somewhat arrogant twist to his face that Danny didn't like at all. His instincts said the prince would be trouble.

The final member of the group stood off the dais and to the king's left. She was the only one with dark hair though that was far from the most remarkable thing about her. Her eyes were almond shaped, golden, and glowed faintly. The tips of her pointed ears poked out from her hair. She had to be at least six feet tall, flat as an ironing board, and dressed in leather armor. A sword hung at her left hip.

Eve stopped three feet from the dais and started to bow. As soon as she did, Danny's body acted without him thinking. His right foot went back, his left arm tucked under his chest, and his right hand swept left to right as he bowed.

Where the hell had that come from? A memory from his host for sure, but damn, he didn't like his body acting on its own like that.

"Raise your heads and be welcome," said someone, the king he assumed.

Danny straightened and assumed parade rest, hands clasped behind his back, feet shoulder width apart. The familiar pose calmed him a little and he figured if he treated the king like he would a general, everything would be fine.

"Eve, welcome," the king said. "And this must be our new hero. I regret the necessity of our meeting. Won't you introduce yourself?"

"Sir! Smith, Daniel J., Lance Corporal, North American Alliance Expeditionary Marines, sir!"

The king leaned back in his throne, a frown creasing his face. "That's quite an introduction. I've never heard one like it. Could you explain?"

Now it was Danny's turn to frown. "My name is Daniel J. Smith. My rank is lance corporal. And I'm a soldier in the North American Alliance Expeditionary Marines. Did you wish to know something else, sir?"

"Yes, perhaps you could clear up a few things for me. You see, according to our histories, the previous heroes all had certain things in common. First, they were all summoned from a place on your world called the Empire of the Rising Sun, but you mentioned a different location."

"Yes, sir. The North American Alliance and the empire are part of a large group of allied nations. We have a military base in the empire and I was stationed there when Eve ripped my soul from my body and brought it here."

The king had the good grace to wince. Danny shouldn't have phrased it like that, but he was still pissed.

"I see," the king said. "So you were in the empire, but born elsewhere. Next, may I ask your age? The previous heroes were all between fifteen and eighteen, hence the age of your host body."

"I was twenty-two."

"Not a huge difference I suppose. You mentioned you were a soldier. Have you fought in many battles?"

"Enough. More than I care to remember. Eve tells me you expect me to fight a bunch more. That right?"

Eve grabbed his sleeve and hissed, "Daniel."

Even as Danny's anger built, something, he had to assume it was memories of his host body, was screaming for him to behave himself. But he didn't want to behave himself. He'd lost everything because of these people. He wanted to scream and rage and punch someone in the face.

"Mind your tongue when you speak to my father," the prince said.

Danny turned his rage on the prince, who flinched back. If ever a face had needed punching, the prince's did.

The king stood and raised his hands. "You're upset. Perfectly understandable given the circumstances of your arrival. And here I am rudely interrogating you. Please accept my apologies for that. You must understand that our scouts have spotted the demon king's forces approaching through Fell Forest. Just advance units, but it won't be long before the bulk of their army arrives."

Danny took a deep breath and let it out over a slow five count. His pulse slowed. The circumstances were what they were. He could hate it all he wanted, but as best he could tell, he was stuck here.

"You're right, I am angry, but anger is a useless emotion. My drill sergeant said all it's good for is getting you killed."

"Why don't we get you settled and meet again in the morning?" the king said. "When I say the enemy will arrive soon, I mean in months, not weeks or days."

Danny nodded. He liked the sound of that idea. "Could I have a tour of the castle? I'd like to move around a bit, get more used to this body."

"Splendid idea. This is going to be your home for the foreseeable future, you might as well have a look around." The king pointed at Lady Shael. "Lyra, why don't you—"

"No!" Danny said. "Not the elf. Anyone but her."

Lyra's eyes crinkled but she remained silent.

"I'll show him around, Father," the younger princess said.

"Excellent, Claudette, thank you. Once you're finished, you know where his room is."

"Of course." Princess Claudette hopped down from the dais and walked over to Danny, a bright smile on her perfect face. "Shall we?"

"By all means."

Danny followed the beautiful princess out of the throne room. Hopefully the fresh air would cool his still-burning temper.

# CHAPTER 4

E ve couldn't say Daniel's outburst surprised her.
The new hero clearly harbored a great deal of
anger at his summoners. She hoped that once he
accepted his new situation his attitude would improve.
Princess Claudette would no doubt do her best to help the
process along.

Deep furrows covered King Richard's brow as he rested
his head in the palm of his hand. He was clearly troubled by
Daniel's outburst. Though he couldn't be shocked by it.

At last he turned his gaze on Eve. "What happened with
the spell?"

Eve cocked her head. "Majesty?"

"The histories all say that the ritual summons a youth in
his mid to late teens from the Empire of the Rising Sun, not a
grown man from another nation. What went wrong?"

Oh, dear. The king must not understand how the spell
worked. "Ah, no, you see the spell is designed as follows. It will
summon the individual in the empire with the highest potential

to interact with the magic of our world. That's it. No mention is made of age, sex, or nationality. When I activated it, Daniel fit the criteria and was summoned. That he was older, male, and not native to the country had no bearing on the spell."

"You should punish him for his attitude," Prince Florian said. "Letting him speak to you in such a way will set a bad precedent."

The king snorted. "Brilliant idea, son. The only man capable of defeating the demon king already hates us for summoning him here. No doubt twenty lashes will have him thinking better of us in short order. Why do you think the royal family meets with the hero for the first time in private? Exactly for outbursts like this. It's happened before. Did you not read the histories? What am I paying that tutor of yours for if you're still this stupid?"

The prince's jaw bunched but he remained silent. Wisely, Eve thought.

King Richard turned to Lady Shael. "What did you think of him, Lyra?"

She shrugged. "Too soon to say. The ether burns bright around him. His potential is every bit as enormous as the past heroes'. Unless the current demon king is far stronger than the earlier ones, with proper training he'll be able to do what needs to be done."

Eve relaxed a bit. If Lady Shael said Daniel could do it, then there was no question he could. Even if he was different from the previous heroes, he carried the same potential. Adonael hadn't led her astray.

"So what do we do now?" Prince Florian asked. "Just let Claudette handle him? If she has her way, they'll be screwing behind the hedges before noon."

"Watch your mouth," the queen said. "That's your sister you're talking about, not some street whore."

"Come on. Don't pretend you're unaware that she's bedded half the nobility along with a big chunk of the royal guard. Adding a notch on her bedpost for the hero is exactly what Claudette is likely to do."

Eve's cheeks burned. Even if the rumors about the younger princess were true, he shouldn't be talking about her behavior so candidly in mixed company. Or any company for that matter. Certain things were better left unspoken.

"If Claudette can calm him down and better yet give him a reason to want to protect our country, I don't care how she does it," King Richard said. "For now, we'll leave the new hero in peace. Let him acclimate and settle in to his new home. Lyra can do his formal analysis tomorrow as well as run him through some drills to see if the host body's memories have properly taken hold. Eventually we'll have a parade to introduce him to the populace. A few thousand cheering and waving people is bound to inflate his ego and make him want to protect the kingdom. Beyond that I'm making no plans. We'll have to take things as they come. Eve."

She jumped when he said her name. "Majesty?"

"I'll be counting on you to handle his education. Only what he needs to know, understand? Keep him focused on the mission."

"Of course, Majesty. That's my duty as Adonael's chosen priestess."

His frown smoothed and some of the worry seemed to lift off his shoulders. "I know. We are all most grateful for everything that the archangels' followers do. Let's call it a day. I can't say our first meeting with the hero went as well as I'd hoped, but there was no violence and he didn't smash any holes in the wall, so it wasn't the worst first meeting in the history of hero summonings."

Eve considered that a pretty low bar to clear, but she understood the sentiment. Despite the bad start, she was confident Daniel would become the hero they needed him to be. At least, for all their sakes, she hoped he would.

○

**B**ehind the castle was an elaborate garden featuring topiary, white gravel paths, fountains, and flowers of all sorts. Danny didn't usually go in for this sort of thing, but today he found the splash of water and gentle breeze perfumed with the scent of flowers soothing.

He shouldn't have lost his temper. Such an outburst was unbecoming of a Marine. Despite knowing that, he couldn't shake his anger completely. These people were in trouble, but that didn't give them the right to kidnap, or soulnap, someone and drag them away from everything they knew and everyone they loved.

Desperate times and desperate measures, he supposed. If he really had no way home, he might not have a choice about fighting the demon king or whatever it was. Having his new home burned to the ground around his ears didn't appeal to him. Well, maybe a little, if he was being honest.

A soft cough drew his attention to the stunning young woman walking along beside him. He thought of her as young, but he was pretty sure she was around the same age as his host body. "You're awfully quiet."

"Busy mind. Plus, I'm not sure how to talk to a princess. You're the first one I've ever met."

"Then don't think of me as a princess. Think of me as a regular woman. I'm sure you must have questions about this world. I'm happy to answer them if I can."

"Even if you weren't a princess, you certainly wouldn't be regular. Why don't you tell me about the region. What's it like when there isn't a demon king?"

"Peaceful and busy. We usually have a hundred or so years between appearances. It takes about half that time to rebuild from the previous war. My grandfather thought he was going to be the one to welcome you and lead the army, but he died ten years ago and there was still no sign of the demon king. According to the histories, this is the longest gap between appearances at one hundred and forty-five years."

"Why the bigger gap?" Danny asked.

"No one knows. Why do the demon lords do any of the mad things they do?"

That was a question asked by many and answered by none. "Do you enjoy history?"

"It's not my favorite thing, but I have a tutor that visits three days a week to give my brother and me lessons. History is a big one. Along with etiquette, diplomacy, calligraphy, and mathematics. Florian also gets lessons in strategy and combat. As a princess I'm spared those last two, though instead I'm expected to attend tea parties with vapid noble girls. Sometimes I wonder if it's a fair trade."

Danny couldn't begin to answer her question. He'd never been to a tea party, much less one with nobility. "Why do you have an elf overseeing the training of heroes?"

"Lyra's only a quarter elf, the last of the quarter-bloods as far as we know. She could beat an entire squad of knights all by herself. She's the strongest wizard and the strongest sword fighter in the kingdom, possibly in the whole world. Or she was before the demon king appeared and we summoned you. Now she's number three."

Danny held up his hand and made a fist. "I don't feel strong. Just making this body work takes a lot of concentration. If I have to work that hard to make a fist, how will I be able to fight?"

"Be patient. You need time to get used to your new body." She grabbed his arm and pressed her considerable assets against him. "I can think of a way to help you get used to moving your body."

No tingle ran through him at the prospect of sleeping with her. That more than anything confirmed how disconnected he was from his body. He also thought of Suzy. Had she gotten the news of his death yet? Probably not, it had only been a few hours. He was stuck here and would never see her again, but he wasn't ready to let go yet.

"I'm flattered, Princess, but as I said, not all of my parts are working properly yet."

To his absolute shock she stopped in the middle of the path and grabbed his crotch. "You're right. This has never been a problem for me before. You do like girls, right?"

"I certainly do." He gently pried her hand loose. "In fact, I was about to ask one to marry me before Eve brought me here."

"Really? Wow, you're definitely older than the other heroes I read about. What was she like?"

Danny let out a long sigh. What was Suzy like? He wasn't sure where to begin. "She's smart, funny, beautiful, sweet. Everything you could ever want in a girlfriend or wife. She's a senior at Sentinel State studying chemistry. She used to try and tell me about it, but the details went way over my head.

Still, I liked to listen to how excited she got about her favorite subjects. It wasn't like I could tell her about my job. Your girlfriend has no desire to hear about your most recent near-death experience. She worried enough as it was."

"Being a soldier is difficult, I imagine. Since I'm not your girlfriend, would you like to tell me about it?"

"Not sure it's suitable for a princess. I've been shot twice, stabbed once, blown up once, and had more close calls than I care to think about. Three years in and out of the sandbox and somehow I made it back to base alive only to die outside a jewelry store with an engagement ring in my pocket. That's life in a nutshell I guess. When you're at your highest it can't wait to kick you in the head."

"You sound rather bitter."

"Wouldn't you be if our situations were reversed?"

She cocked her head as if deep in thought. "I suppose I would. The truth is I'd never really thought about what it meant to be summoned. The ritual is something you read about in books, not something you consider deeply."

"Yeah, I suppose you wouldn't. Could you show me the kitchen next? I need a bite to eat."

Claudette smiled. "Of course, it's about lunchtime anyway."

Danny followed her back toward the castle. His mind was still all over the place, but the worst of the anger was gone. Clear thinking was going to be vital if he wanted to get through this mess alive.

○

Richard took a deep breath, blew it out, and tried to relax. He'd traded the throne room for his private chambers. He sank into a soft leather chair and worked his neck from side to side. Why in heaven's name couldn't the demon king have appeared during Father's reign? Picking up the pieces after the war would've been awful, but so much less awful than having to deal with the hero and fight the demon king's army.

Daniel was not at all what Richard was expecting. He had far too much life experience to be easily manipulated, far too much power to be coerced, and far too much anger to be forced to do anything. Hopefully Claudette could find more pleasant ways to motivate him. She had a knack for it assuming even half the rumors were true. Having a well-known slut for a daughter was embarrassing, but she balanced it out by bringing him all sorts of useful information gleaned from her lovers. All in all, he considered it a draw.

And if it could help keep Daniel in line, he didn't care what acts she had to perform.

Someone knocked. Since he'd dismissed all the servants, Richard had to stand and open the door himself. He found Claudette outside, not rumpled in the least.

"Come in." She flounced past him and dropped into one of the other leather chairs. "How'd it go?"

"Not as well as I would've liked. His dick isn't working yet and he had a sweetheart back on his world. One he was preparing to marry from the sounds of it. I'm guessing he still feels a strong connection to her. He's not going to be a quick tumble, more's the pity."

That was a more graphic description than Richard would've preferred but he got the idea. "Did he tell you anything useful? Anything we might use to keep him loyal to the mission? I haven't mentioned the hero's mansion or any sort of reward."

"Not really. He's quite bitter about the whole thing and I can't blame him. If I was in his position, taken from my world and everyone I knew then told, 'oh yeah, you also have to fight a demon king,' I doubt I'd be thrilled either."

Richard let out a little growl. "You're supposed to be on my side, not sympathizing with the hero. Maybe Lyra will have better luck."

"I wouldn't count on it. He didn't say it outright, but Daniel clearly hates elves."

"Elf-bloods," Richard corrected automatically.

"Whatever. You know what I mean."

"I do. Where is he now?"

Claudette's face twisted into something ugly. "The dining hall. I handed him off to Eve. With any luck the perfect priestess will get better results than I did."

Richard had no idea what his daughter had against Eve and it didn't matter. "As long as someone does, I don't care who it is."

All he needed was a hero sufficiently compliant and skilled to kill the demon king and not cause any irreparable harm in the process. Whether it was Claudette's body or Eve's earnestness that convinced him, Richard would be thrilled with anything that worked.

# CHAPTER 5

When Danny woke it was still dark outside his window. Not surprising considering how early he went to bed. The royal family had provided him with a suite of three rooms. None of which was a bathroom. A bronze pan with a lid handled that role. And the less said about the scraps of rough cloth which served as toilet paper the better.

At least his body appeared to be working properly as he rolled out of the deep feather bed. A few calisthenics, starting with jumping jacks and ending with sit-ups, got his blood pumping. His usual nightmares hadn't been as bad last night. He still saw the faces of all the men he'd killed, but they were muted, like he was seeing them through a window smeared with jelly. He imagined his new body had something to do with it. If so, it was the first thing he'd found to be grateful for.

Exercises done, he went to the dressing table, poured water from the pitcher into a basin and washed up. There was no toothbrush, so he used his finger and some water. Far from ideal, but in such a primitive place you had to make the best of it. It was like camping only you forgot all your supplies.

He tied his hair back, pulled his boots on, and opened the door. A sound-asleep guard leaned against the wall opposite his room. Good to know he had such dedicated warriors overseeing his security.

With a shrug he turned toward the dining room. He'd gotten a solid feel for the castle layout when Eve showed him around after lunch yesterday. He found the sweet-natured priestess much easier to deal with than the far sexier Claudette. Danny figured it would be wise to avoid the second princess for the time being. Danny wasn't sure how he felt about her suggestions and needed some time to make his peace with the fact that he was never going to see Suzy again.

Shouldn't be an issue today anyway. The last thing Eve said before bringing him to his room was that he should meet the elf woman as soon as he was set in the morning. She was supposed to analyze him, whatever the hell that meant. The king had said something about a meeting as well, but no one gave Danny any details.

He walked down the quiet halls, expecting to meet someone at any moment and being consistently disappointed. Everyone must still be asleep. Still, you'd think some of the servants would be up and about.

A whiff of something tasty caught his attention and hastened his footsteps. He had to be getting close to the kitchen. Sure enough he found the dining room a moment later along with about forty soldiers and a dozen servants scattered around the wooden tables.

Everyone stared at Danny when he entered. It wasn't a

comfortable feeling.

"Morning. I was hoping to have some breakfast. Please enjoy your meals. Pretend I'm not here."

Of course that was never going to happen. A woman in a red smock covered by a white apron sprang to her feet and hurried over. "Please, Hero, have a seat. I'll get you whatever you'd like. In fact, there should've been someone outside your room to bring you breakfast."

He allowed himself to be led to an empty table and sat. "There was a sleeping guard outside, but I hated to wake him. I am perfectly capable of getting my own breakfast."

"Of course you are. What would you like?"

There was no point arguing with her. "A plate of whatever you're all having is fine. It smells wonderful. And a mug of whatever the guards are drinking, please."

"Don't be silly, that's servant food. The cook will make you whatever you want I'm sure."

Danny smiled in the hope that he might calm the anxious woman. "I'm used to army food, ma'am. Whatever you're having will be fine, I promise."

She seemed to decide arguing with him would be ruder than feeding him servant food so she bustled off to collect it.

Danny turned to the guards. "Morning. Where are you guys stationed?"

They all looked at each other as if uncertain whether it was okay to talk to him. Finally one of them said, "We're the wall guards, my lord. We man the gate and patrol the ramparts. Our shift starts at dawn."

"Some of you must have been on duty when Eve brought me here yesterday. I apologize for not recognizing you. I was a bit out of it when we arrived."

"Not a problem, my lord. No one pays us any mind."

Danny had done his share of guard duty and felt that hard. Before he could continue the conversation, such as it was, the servant returned with a loaded plate and a mug. All of which she placed in front of Danny.

"Here you are, my lord. I hope it suits you."

"I'm sure it will and please, call me Daniel."

She blanched. "I couldn't possibly."

With a curtsy, she fled back to her table.

Danny swallowed a sigh. He didn't especially like having everyone nervous around him. He wasn't a big shot and disliked being treated as one. Well, like it or not, being the hero meant he was a big shot, here at least.

Putting thoughts of status out of his mind, he set to eating what he'd have called a hash back home. Fried potatoes made up the bulk of it, along with bits of meat that resembled bacon, some onions or leeks, and a fried egg on top. It was delicious. Only the weak, sour wine was a disappointment. But as breakfasts went, it was above average.

Now, where did he take his plate?

He stood, plate and mug in hand. Well, they were in hand for the half a minute it took the same servant to collect them and carry them away.

"Can any of you tell me where I'm supposed to be analyzed?"

"You should go back and wake up your guard," said the man he'd spoken with earlier. "Have him take you. If you show up without him, he's liable to receive a whipping."

That sounded excessive, but Danny nodded. "Thanks, I'll do that. Hopefully you have a quiet day on duty."

"Every day on castle duty is quiet. Your arrival yesterday was the most exciting thing to happen since I was assigned to this post."

Danny grinned as he stood. "Let's hope it stays that way."

He left the dining room and retraced his steps. He'd always had an excellent sense of direction, so finding his way back to his room was simple enough. When he arrived, the guard was still snoring happily away.

Much as he hated to do it, Danny really wanted to get whatever was going to happen today over with, so he gave the guard a shake. The man's eyes popped open, he stared at Danny for a moment, then scrambled to straighten up and salute all at the same time. He succeeded in getting tangled up in his own feet and ended up on his backside.

"Forgive me, my lord. I didn't mean to fall asleep. Please don't mention it to the guard captain. I don't know what he might do."

"Relax, your secret's safe with me. But I do need you to show me the way to wherever I'm supposed to meet the elf."

"Right, you're having your formal analysis today. Lady Shael likes to work outside, so she'll be in the training yard." The guard set off down the hall, the opposite way from the dining hall. "Assuming she's arrived at the castle anyway. It's still early. It is still early, isn't it?"

"The sun hadn't risen when I did and that was about half an hour ago. Does she not live in the castle?"

"No, she lives on a large estate a little ways outside the city with her granddaughters. That's what she calls them. Truth is they're orphans she adopted. Elf-bloods. No human family wanted them so they ended up with her."

"Are elves disliked in the kingdom?" Danny could certainly understand if they were. Everyone from his world certainly hated them. "I can't imagine they would be, given her high status."

"No, not disliked exactly. They're so long lived it makes

them hard to deal with. Like, if you adopt an elf kid, he's not going to grow up during your lifetime. Elves are considered children until they're a hundred and adolescents until two hundred. I can't imagine dealing with a teenager for a hundred years."

"How old is Lady Shael?" Danny asked.

"Around fifteen hundred, I think. She was here before the first hero was summoned over a thousand years ago."

"Holy shit."

"Yes, sir. That pretty well sums it up. She's forgot more about magic than most humans will ever learn."

They rounded a corner and Danny nodded to a pair of servant girls carrying baskets of clean laundry, dressed like the older woman who waited on him that morning. They quickly turned away from him. He sighed.

"Everyone seems jumpy around me. Is the hero someone they're meant to be afraid of?"

"Not afraid, sir. You're basically a noble in the kingdom. There are certain things folks like us don't do around folks like you. Looking you in the eye and talking being at the top of the list."

"You're doing okay."

"I'm answering your questions, sir. If a noble asks a question you'd best answer double quick. Not you, sir, but me and the other servants."

"I figured, thanks." Danny rubbed his face. He didn't know shit about being noble and he didn't enjoy being treated like one. Not that he expected his wishes would change anything. "Tell me about this analyzing business."

"It's real easy, sir. Citizens of the Five Kingdoms have their magical potential measured at the age of thirteen. It helps determine what jobs you qualify for, that sort of thing.

I haven't got enough potential to light a candle. I'm sure you'll do better."

Sounded like the test Danny took his senior year of high school. The little meter the snotty department wizard made him touch hadn't reacted to him at all. Not that he or anyone else had expected it to since he was a man. Of course, they thought the same thing the next year when Conryu Koda took the test and see how that turned out.

They left the castle and crunched down a gravel path to a dirt training ground about the size of a football field. The sun was rising and it painted the sky in shades of red and orange. That usually meant bad weather coming.

His guide made a little circle above his head.

"What's that about?" Danny asked.

"Adonael's halo symbol, it's to ward off bad luck. A demon sky is never a good thing. Lady Shael is over yonder. Best of luck, sir."

Danny looked where his guide pointed and finally spotted the elf's slender figure. He took a step toward her then turned back. "Sorry, I didn't catch your name. I'm Daniel."

"Albert, sir. Thank you for asking." He said it like he was French: *Al Bear.*

"Thank you for the info. If you want to take a nap, I imagine I'll be a while."

"I'm up and at 'em now, sir, never fear."

Danny nodded and strode toward the elf. He needed to keep his anger in check. She hadn't invaded his world personally and it wasn't fair to hate her for being the same race as those who had.

He tried to make himself believe it and failed miserably.

# CHAPTER 6

D anny stomped over to where the elf waited. No, not the elf. Lyra. She had a name and he needed to start thinking of her that way. Anyway, he made enough noise to be sure he didn't startle her. Not that he had to worry. He only managed three strides before she turned to face him, watching him approach with her creepy glowing eyes. Her leather armor fit her slim body perfectly, allowing freedom of movement while protecting all the vital points.

He stopped three feet away and clasped his hands behind his back. "Ma'am, reporting for analysis."

"For this to work, I have to touch you. Is that going to be a problem?" Lyra's voice was high, but with a perfect pitch. She could've been an opera singer on Earth.

"No, ma'am. I apologize for my outburst yesterday. Elves invaded my world long ago. They killed many of my ancestors and I guess I harbored bad feelings for the entire race. You can't be blamed for the actions of a bunch of other elves."

"Though I was only a child at the time, those were my kin

who invaded your world. I deeply regret their actions, please believe that."

Danny stared at her. "Wait, the elves that invaded Earth actually came from here?"

Lyra nodded. "They forged the link between our worlds which allows the summoning ritual to work. For better or worse, your Earth and Valindor are permanently connected in the ether."

Danny was having a bit of trouble processing what she said. The timeframe lined up, but the idea that the two worlds were still connected seemed impossible. Though, given Danny's limited understanding of magic, maybe he was surprised by something that made perfect sense.

He was going to have to get used to the idea that some things simply worked the way they worked without a rational explanation. He rarely had to deal with magic on Earth and so wasn't used to it. For now, it was time to move things along.

"Do what you have to. I'm ready when you are."

Lyra took a single step and placed the tip of her right index finger on his forehead. A moment later it grew a little warm. She held it there for a thirty count, then stepped back. Danny felt nothing through the entire process.

"That wasn't so bad. Do I pass?"

"More than pass. Of all the heroes I've analyzed, you are the strongest." Her voice held a slight quaver and the hand that had touched him trembled.

"That's good, right?"

"It is, but it also makes me wonder if this demon king is so much stronger than the last one that we should need a hero as strong as you. It's an alarming thought."

Yeah, no shit. Especially since he was going to have to

fight the guy. "Okay, you've analyzed me, what happens now?"

"Now we start your training. All the combat and magical skills you'll need already reside in your body's memory. The key is to make them part of you so you can use them like they are your own. And that will take practice. The most basic skill is circulating ether through your body. This will make you faster, stronger, and more durable than a normal man. This group of techniques is called physical enhancement. Are you ready to try?"

Danny wasn't at all sure he was, but he nodded anyway. He'd best learn to defend himself with swords and sorcery. He doubted anyone was going to drop an M16 in his lap, so he had to rely on this magic nonsense.

"Picture the ether flowing through your body. Some picture light, others a mist. For this technique, it doesn't matter what form your visualization takes, it only needs to make sense for you. Eventually you'll be able to use it without conscious thought."

He thought back to how he felt when he nearly killed Eve. "Would fire work? Like heat spreading through my body?"

"It should work as well as anything else. Why did you choose that visualization?"

Danny explained what happened in the cathedral. "It felt like liquid fire running through my veins. It was the damnedest thing I've ever experienced."

"Remarkable. Your weakened soul called on the ether instinctively. That's a first in my experience. Show me what you did."

Danny tried to remember the feeling without the anger. He didn't want to lose control again. The thought barely formed when the flames came racing through him. It was a rush and terrifying all at the same time. He turned toward Lyra and found the elf staring at him with a hand to her mouth.

Shit. Did he screw up that badly already? "What?"

"How can you be alive while channeling so much ether? A human body should've been blown apart in an instant. Even a half-elf of the high council would struggle to contain so much energy."

"I don't know what to tell you. I feel a little warm but otherwise I'm fine. I just did what you told me to. Um, is this a good thing or a bad thing?" He seemed to be asking that question a lot.

"Too soon to say. It could potentially be either. Come with me, we need to test a few things." Lyra moved to go deeper into the training ground.

Danny took a step and pushed his foot into the ground up to his ankle. "Little help."

She turned back. "What did you do?"

"Nothing, I swear. I took a step to follow you and when I pressed my foot down this happened. It's going to be a problem if I can't walk while I'm powered up."

"It certainly will be. For now pull your foot out."

Danny jerked his foot up, sending a clod of dirt and gravel flying and leaving a six-inch-deep, one-foot-diameter divot in the path. "If you have a shovel I can fix that."

Lyra appeared to be stifling laughter. Swell, at least someone found his predicament amusing.

"Don't worry, the groundskeepers will take care of it. That's their job after all. Now follow me, gently this time."

Gently. Okay, he could do this. Just imagine he was sneaking up on an enemy lookout. He'd done that plenty of times.

He took a step and his foot didn't sink in. He wanted to thrust a fist into the air, but feared what might happen if he did. In fact, not only did his foot not sink in, but the gravel didn't so much as crunch when he stepped on it.

"What did you do now?" she asked.

"I'm walking gently, like you said."

Lyra shook her head. "What are you picturing?"

He explained about the lookout and she sighed. "What? What the hell have I done wrong this time?"

"You haven't done anything wrong exactly, but you're so tightly connected to the ether at the moment that your every thought is acting like a spell. You've conjured a stealth bubble around yourself. It's absorbing every sound you make. Your feet aren't touching the ground, thus no tracks. I'm surprised you haven't turned yourself invisible while you were at it."

"When I'm sneaking up on a target, I don't picture myself as invisible because in my world it's not possible for me to become invisible, only stealthy and quiet." His brow furrowed as he imagined himself vanishing completely from view. "How about now?"

For a moment Lyra looked as old as she was supposed to be. "Yes, you're now invisible as well. Clearly using magic is not going to be an issue for you. Controlling it, on the other hand, is going to be a bigger problem than I feared. Release the energy, all of it."

Danny frowned. She made it sound simple, but the first time he did it, there'd been no thought involved. He'd been so horrified about nearly killing Eve that it sort of happened on its own. Pulling the power in had been easy, pushing it out should be equally easy. All he had to do was visualize what he wanted and the magic would oblige.

Okay, he could do this. He imagined the fire in his veins

draining out until the heat had left his body. He opened his eyes and found himself standing in a circle of blackened earth.

"Well, you did it, more or less."

"Yeah. I guess picturing the fire draining out of me isn't the best visualization."

"Your assessment is correct. And now you know why we train outside. Are you well?"

Danny checked himself over. He hadn't burned his clothes off and nothing hurt. All in all, he couldn't complain. "I'm fine, I guess. Why?"

"If an ordinary wizard had tried to wield as much ether as you did, it would've killed him. If they reached their maximum and held it for as long as you did, they'd be in a coma for days if not weeks. You did it like it was nothing. That implies you weren't even close to your maximum. The thought terrifies me."

If Danny had understood exactly what she was talking about, he felt certain he'd be scared as well. As things stood, he was just nervous and confused. "So what's this experiment you want to conduct?"

"I'm a little hesitant about trying it now, but we're practicing on dummies, so it should be fine."

She led him to a row of wooden posts which had crossbars nailed to the top with round shields hanging from them. "The knights use these to practice swordsmanship. Mostly by doing forms over and over again to build up their strength. I want you to hit a shield, once on your own and once when channeling your magic. I'm hoping to see how much it increases your strength."

She handed him a battered sword that had been leaning against one of the posts. Nicks covered the edge and the blade had a slight bend, but otherwise it looked sturdy enough.

Danny stepped up to the nearest post. When he did, another memory overtook him and his stance adjusted like he was a puppet under his host's control. It was one of the more disconcerting things he'd ever experienced and he would be perfectly happy if it never happened again. Finally he swung; legs, hips, and shoulders driving his arm forward to slam into the round shield with a rousing clang.

When he recovered, he instantly knew exactly how to do that move again as well as a number of other training moves. This must have been what Eve was talking about when she mentioned his memories needing permission to work.

"Not bad. Your technique was perfect. Now do it again while you channel the ether. I want you to hit it as hard as you can, no holding back."

Danny frowned. "You sure? Considering what happened before, don't you think I ought to hold back a little bit?"

"No. I need to see what I'm working with. We'll practice your modulation later."

She was the instructor. If that was what she wanted, he'd give it his best shot.

The instant he thought of the fire he found his body blazing with it. The power came far faster this time. He tightened his grip on the ragged sword and the handle cracked under his fingers. Yikes. No way would this piece of junk survive a full-power hit. Not unless he did something to make it stronger.

No sooner did he think that than the fire, as he'd come to think of it, flowed down his hand to cover the sword. He couldn't see the energy—what did she call it? The ether—but he felt it. He knew it had done what he wanted. Exactly how he knew it, he'd worry about later.

Weapon reinforced, he gathered himself and swung. No weird memories butted in this time. The stroke felt perfectly natural.

What happened to the target was anything but. Mr. Postman exploded out of the ground and flew all the way across the training ground. It probably would've kept going, only it slammed into the castle wall with enough force to shatter the wood.

She said she wanted him to give it all he had and Danny was pretty sure he'd done so. This time he pictured the magic evaporating like steam. It drained out, doing no damage to his surroundings.

Lyra stood beside him and shook her head.

"Not what you were expecting?"

"More than I was expecting actually. I'm impressed you managed to enhance the sword as well. I never thought to mention it."

"The handle cracked when I squeezed it so I figured if I didn't want to send shrapnel downrange I'd best do something."

"Indeed, it was the correct decision. The force of your blow impressed me greatly. Once we add control, finesse, and experience, you'll be an unstoppable swordsman. Congratulations, your assessment is complete. We can now begin proper sword training." Danny grimaced so she quickly added, "The basics won't take long. You only need to go through the routines a couple times to unlock your memories. We should have that done by the end of the day."

"What about my meeting with the king?"

"This is more important. We'll finish the basics in the morning, then we can move on to sparring."

"Is that safe?" He gave the smashed post a meaningful look.

"It will be, as long as you don't use your magic. If you can trust me to lead you down the correct path, this will go much more smoothly."

Danny nodded. He wasn't much on trust, but he knew how to follow orders. He figured it would be like going through basic training again. He'd survived it once, he could do it again.

○

Lyra watched Daniel go through sword forms, smoothly shifting stances, altering the course of his blade, and generally looking like he'd been studying swordsmanship his whole life. It never ceased to amaze her how the host body's skills could remain so sharp despite having a new soul. The previous six heroes she trained all showed similar results, but none so quickly.

The difference between her current student and her previous ones lay in their ability to focus. Once he got started, Daniel had worked for hours nonstop without complaints or missing a beat. If she hadn't believed his stated age, she certainly did now. It had always been clear to her when dealing with the other heroes that they were, in the end, children. Powerful, dangerous children, but children nonetheless.

Despite the necessity, she had always felt guilty about turning innocent children into warriors. It was wrong on so many levels, but to save the many, their innocence had to be sacrificed.

The sun was starting to set when Lyra said, "That's enough for today."

Daniel made a final swing that cut the air with a whoosh then set his sword back where he'd found it. Somehow the weapon didn't disintegrate after all the abuse it had taken.

"How do you feel?" Lyra asked.

"Hungry, but otherwise fine. The movements are more natural now and the memories haven't stabbed my brain for a few hours."

"Excellent, the lack of psychic reaction means the skills are fully yours now. Tomorrow you'll spar with the first-year knights. No magic, just some semi-realistic combat. Depending on how it goes, I'll decide the next step for your training."

Daniel nodded, back straight and hands clasped behind his back as he watched her. He adopted that pose in the throne room as well. None of the other heroes had ever done anything similar. They tended to bow a lot.

"Was there anything else, ma'am? I'd like to see about dinner."

"No, my mind drifted for a moment. The other heroes used to call me Sensei."

Daniel smiled, not an expression she'd seen on his face before. "I'm not surprised. An Imperial kid would certainly consider you his teacher and use that as a term of respect. My school days are long behind me and even if they weren't, where I went to school we called our teacher by their last name. So you'd be Mrs. Shael. Or is it Ms. Shael?"

Lyra wasn't familiar with either of those honorifics. "What's the difference?"

"The first one is if you're married and the second is if you're single."

"I see, the latter then. Go enjoy your dinner."

"Yes, ma'am. Same time tomorrow?"

She nodded and he turned and marched away, his guard falling in beside him.

Lyra had her doubts about whether she and Daniel would ever enjoy the sort of close rapport she'd had with the other heroes, and that was fine. A working relationship that left him properly trained and the demon king defeated was more than enough.

Speaking of working relationships, King Richard expected an update after their first session. Lyra didn't especially like the human king, though he was better than some of the men she'd been forced to deal with over her long life. For all his faults, this one at least didn't think her responsibilities extended to his bedroom.

She left the training yard and made her way through the castle. Servants paused and bowed to her as she passed. The way they trembled made it clear they acted out of fear rather than respect. That was fine with her. All she wanted from the bulk of humanity was to be left alone.

Only the needs of her people kept her here, serving the human kings, and training the heroes. The latter especially required her help. There was no one else, human or elvish, with the knowledge and experience to train someone as mighty as the heroes. If a human wizard or arcane knight tried, they'd be apt to get themselves killed.

At last she arrived at the door to the royal suite. There were no guards this deep in the castle, so she knocked herself. A moment later the eldest princess opened the door. She started a bit when she saw Lyra, but that wasn't unusual.

Unlike her free-spirited sister, Princess Clara was a prim, nervous young woman who seldom spoke unless directly asked a question. At least that's how she acted when Lyra was around. Perhaps she relaxed around girls her own age.

"Is the king available?" Lyra asked. "I finished Daniel's analysis."

"Come in here!" the king bellowed from deeper in the suite.

Clara stepped aside without a word.

Putting the timid princess out of her mind, Lyra strode into the suite and found the king and queen seated together at the dining table, a spread of food laid out between them.

"Hungry?" King Richard asked. "Take a seat and join us."

She sat, but only helped herself to a glass of wine and some grapes. Roast beef covered in gravy was too rich for her tastes. Whatever else you might say about humans, the people of this country had a gift for fermenting grapes.

"So, can he do the job? You're still alive, so I'm guessing you didn't come to blows."

"No, Majesty, we didn't. Daniel was much calmer today. Whether or not he's fully accepted his destiny as the hero, I'm less certain, but he followed my instructions without issue, so that was a solid start. As for your first question, I can say with complete confidence that Daniel is the strongest hero ever summoned. His raw potential is absolutely staggering."

The king beamed at her. "That's great news. Given his differences from the other heroes, I'd feared he might not measure up. It is great news, right?"

He must have noticed her scowling. "It is, assuming the current demon king isn't equally empowered. My primary fear is that Lady Adonael guided the magic to Daniel specifically because she knew we faced an even graver threat than usual."

"What are the chances of that? Our scouts haven't mentioned seeing any out-of-the-ordinary monsters among the first groups."

"I have no idea, Majesty. As I say, it's my fear and it could be wholly misplaced. In any case, Daniel is the hero we have and I'll do my best to see that he's trained to his maximum potential. Should I succeed in doing so, I can't imagine a demon king strong enough to stand against him."

"Well enough. Where is he now? A meeting was mentioned, but it's getting late."

"Gone to eat his evening meal. We start sparring tomorrow if you'd like to observe."

King Richard took a deep drink of wine and shook his head. "I have meetings with the generals tomorrow. When do you begin his magical training? I'm much more interested in seeing that."

"In a couple more days. But we're going to have to do it outside the city. I don't want to risk an errant spell going out of control where there are other people."

"I see. Well, I hope you can get him sufficiently under control that he can give a demonstration when the Conclave of Kings begins."

"Two weeks isn't a long time, Majesty, but I'll do my best."

"Your best has always been enough and the kingdom appreciates your efforts. I'm sure your people do as well."

Lyra had serious doubts about both of those claims, but she lowered her head in a seated bow of appreciation for his lies. It was the polite thing after all.

# CHAPTER 7

Once again Danny found himself awake and out of bed before the sun rose. It was a habit and his recent redeployment, which was how he'd decided to think of his current situation, hadn't changed anything. Hopefully he could have some more of that hash. He'd discovered yesterday that the people of this kingdom didn't eat lunch, only breakfast and dinner. Had he known, he'd have gotten a bigger plate. He was supposed to be sparring with some knights today which meant he'd need his strength.

Dressed and ready, he opened the door. Albert, bless his heart, was awake to greet him this morning. Apparently he served from midnight until noon then Jean took over for the second shift. Jean hadn't been nearly as chatty as he trudged stoically along at Danny's side. The guards seemed kind of pointless, but he assumed their real job was to keep an eye on the new hero and make sure he didn't end up lost.

"Morning, my lord," Albert said. "Sleep well?"

Danny had, in fact, slept like the dead. He suspected it

was mental exhaustion from having to absorb so many memories. Physically, the training yesterday hadn't been bad at all.

"Yeah, did you?"

Albert winced. "I didn't doze off last night, my lord, I swear."

"Glad to hear it. And knock off the 'my lord' business. 'Sir' is fine if you can't call me Daniel."

"Yes, sir. Shall I fetch you some breakfast?"

"No, I think I'll go eat in the same dining hall as yesterday. The food was tasty even if the people were a bit nervous."

Albert's gaze went anywhere but at him. "Not sure that's the best idea, sir."

"And why not?"

"The powers that be don't want you mixing with the riffraff. Only reason I didn't bring your food yesterday was my napping."

"No one told me and I like eating with people. If the powers that be don't like it, they can go fu... Take a flying leap." He barely cut the vulgar remark off in time. He was trying to be on his best behavior.

Albert shrugged. "If that's your preference, it's not like I could stop you if I wanted to."

"Good, come on."

Danny led the way to the dining room and when they arrived the same group as yesterday was busy enjoying breakfast. Everyone started to stand when he arrived, but he waved them down. "No need to fuss. I just happen to like company when I eat."

"Will you join us, my lord?" one of the guards asked. That

was different. Yesterday they'd hardly looked at him. The change suited Danny very well.

"I will, thanks. Let me grab a plate."

"I'll get one for each of us, sir," Albert said. "You have a seat."

Some arguments weren't worth the effort, so Danny sat beside the guard that invited him over. The rest of the forty or so men at the table still refused to speak or look at him. But no one fled, so he'd call that a win.

"I appreciate the welcome. Everyone appears a bit on edge around me and it's making me uncomfortable. They might call me a hero here, but back home I was a soldier like you. I fought for my country, protected my brothers, and did my best to survive. I was nothing special. Being treated like some kind of nobleman is weird, so if you could act like I'm a fellow soldier, I'd be most grateful."

"We can't do that when any of the higher-ups are around," the chatty guard said. "But we can try at breakfast."

"Thanks." Albert arrived with their food, the same hash as yesterday happily, and Danny dug in.

When he'd eaten a few bites, one of the guards, he didn't catch which one, asked, "Did you see much action, sir?"

"More than I'd like. I was recovering from pretty serious surgery when I got summoned here. I've been wounded in action four times and fought more skirmishes than I can count. Being a Marine is definitely not for the faint of heart. What about you guys?"

They got to trading stories and the guards finally lightened up. They even laughed a couple times. It was different, but the brief camaraderie reminded Danny of the barracks back home. And then it was time for everyone to go to their posts.

The guards and servants went one way while Danny and Albert went the other. As they walked Danny said, "That wasn't so bad, was it?"

"No, sir. Still, I won't be reporting it to my captain."

"As you think best. I don't care one way or the other."

They reached the training yard and found Lyra waiting, but no knights. At least the sky was clear today. They didn't need any more bad omens. Albert stayed well back while Danny went to talk to his instructor.

"Morning, ma'am. I expected to find a knight or two here with you."

"They'll be along. Did you sleep well?" The way she asked suggested she expected a no.

"Yeah, fine. I was exhausted, mentally anyway. I didn't even have nightmares."

"Do you usually?"

"I'd rather not talk about it. So what's the plan for today?"

"Sparring, like I said. You'll use no magic. These are regular knights. Most of them were squires a year ago, so they're not very experienced. Should be a good test for you."

Danny always enjoyed the sparring ring, though the Marines used pugil sticks, not wooden swords. "What about safety gear?"

"There's a leather breastplate and helmet beside the training circle. You can prepare now if you'd like."

Since he'd never worn such things, he figured that might be prudent. Lyra led him to a circle someone had drawn in the dirt. The leather breastplate reminded him a little of the bulletproof vests they wore on patrol. He slipped it over his head and settled it on his shoulders. Buckles on the side rather than hook-and-loop straps tightened it down. The helmet was steel and had a visor with slits that cut off his vision more than he'd like, but the weight wasn't bad.

Finally, he picked up the wooden sword and gave it a couple swings. The heft was similar to the metal one he used yesterday. No doubt intentionally so. Not a terrible bit of kit, all things considered.

Danny had barely done a handful of practice moves when four guys wearing armor like his, wooden swords in one hand, and carrying their helmets under their arms came marching across the training yard from the opposite direction. They were led by an older man with graying blond hair wearing proper steel armor.

"I didn't expect Knight Commander Morel to be joining us," Lyra muttered.

"Is he a problem?" Danny asked.

"He argued, strongly, that he should oversee your combat training while I handled the magic. As if the two were separable when you were training to be a hero. He's not even an arcane knight." She sounded thoroughly disgusted.

"So, is he going to be a problem?" Danny asked again.

"I don't think so, but he might have told his men to go harder on you than I had planned on your first day of sparring."

"This isn't my first time in the circle. If they think I'm easy meat, they've got a surprise coming."

"Lady Shael, Sir Hero," Commander Morel said. "A fine morning for a workout, wouldn't you say?"

He sounded entirely too enthusiastic and Danny mistrusted him at once.

"I was certain you'd have too much on your plate to join us this morning, Alban."

"Nonsense. I wouldn't miss the hero's first sparring match for anything. My reports will keep for a few hours."

Lyra and Alban glared at each other through fake smiles.

Danny glanced at one of the knights, who offered a faint shrug as if to say what can you do? Looked like his underlings weren't enthusiastic about whatever their commander had in store. That couldn't be good for Danny.

Alban clapped his gauntleted hands together. "Shall we begin? Genet, why don't you go first?"

The knight who shrugged when Danny glanced his way stepped into the circle and put his helmet in place. He had a decent build without being oversized. Probably quick too. Exactly the sort of person that would give Danny a hard time. And, assuming Lyra was right, he likely had orders to make the match extra tough.

Time to find out for sure. He stepped into the circle facing Genet.

Alban took a breath to speak but Lyra cut in. "You will obey my orders at all times. When I say the match is over, it's over. No magic is allowed. Failure to obey these rules will be punished. Clear?"

Danny nodded and Genet followed suit.

"On your guard!"

Danny raised his sword to middle guard and memories of many matches assailed him.

"Begin!"

Genet charged, sword leading.

Danny barely avoided the first blow as he fought to order his thoughts. Every move he made awakened new memories. It was impossible to concentrate on the fight.

A hard blow struck his arm and he grimaced. He had no hope of winning at this rate and Genet wasn't giving him a chance to recover. This was supposed to be training for hell's sake. The first couple matches should've been easy so he could integrate more memories.

It seemed the knights had other plans.

Well, Danny could change his plans too.

He gripped the sword in two hands like a pugil stick and lunged straight ahead.

The move took Genet by surprise and he didn't move out of the way. The wooden sword drove hard into his gut. Danny crouched and lifted, sending the knight flying over his back to land hard on the dirt.

A moment later he was on top, pinning Genet to the ground and laying the edge of his sword on his neck.

"Stop!" Lyra said. "The first match is over."

Danny had barely made it to his feet when Lyra rounded on Alban. "What the hell are you playing at? You know it takes time for the hero's soul and the host's memories to unify, yet your subordinate went after Daniel like this was a graduation match. The whole point was for this to be an easy day to facilitate that unification."

Alban scoffed. "Surely the hero can handle a bit of rough training. If he were under my authority, that bout would've been nothing. And what sort of strange training have you been giving him? I've never seen that fighting style."

While the two leaders bickered, Danny turned to Genet. "Is this kind of thing normal?"

"Unfortunately. Sir Morel is an ambitious man and as soon as he heard that the decision had been made to summon the hero, he made up his mind to use you however he could to advance his station. The only way to do that is to separate you from Lady Shael. You know, the immortal elf-blood who successfully trained the six prior heroes."

Genet gave a little shake of his head. "He's not the most reasonable of men. Also, sorry I went after you so hard. Orders."

Danny shrugged. He'd been lucky none of his COs were glory-hungry assholes. There were plenty of less-fortunate units and their attrition rates reflected it.

"Don't worry about it. Everyone answers to somebody."

Genet popped his helmet off and grinned. "Even you?"

"Sort of. It helps when you're the only one able to kill the demon king. I mean, what are they going to do, dismiss me?"

Genet burst out laughing, drawing glares from both Alban and Lyra. At least he got them to stop arguing.

"Are you two finished?" Danny asked. "Got all the kinks worked out of the training regimen? From the sounds of it, we need to move this process along. While I'm not keen on the whole 'fighting the demon king' project, if it has to happen, I'd as soon be properly prepared."

"Who do you think you're talking to, boy?" Alban said. "I'll have you know I'm the most decorated knight in a century and I'll not be spoken to by anyone, hero or otherwise, in such a disrespectful tone."

"No?" Danny asked. "What are you going to do about it? A fantastic knight such as yourself could no doubt handle this demon king problem all on his own. Save me a lot of trouble. Sound like a good plan?"

Alban tried to stare Danny down and Danny stared right back. Blowhard pricks like this weren't useful for much beyond getting better men killed. If he couldn't find a way to be useful, he could get the hell out of the way.

Alban blinked first. "Men, we're leaving. Our efforts will not be appreciated here. I'll be speaking to His Majesty about the hero's lack of respect at the first opportunity. His teacher is clearly a bad influence. Once I'm in charge, boy, I'll teach you some discipline."

And the knights marched back out the way they'd come. His initial round of sparring lasted under twenty minutes. All things considered, not the most promising start to his training.

"Alban's a fool, but a powerful one," Lyra said. "You've made an enemy today."

Danny shrugged. "Like I said to Genet, what are they going to do, fire me? Unless you can summon another hero, I'm pretty sure I can say whatever I want, especially if it's the truth. I've seen people like him often enough to know the best thing the king could do is give him a job with lots of titles and as far from anything important as possible."

"It's not so simple. His brother is Duke Morel, one of the most feared members of the nobility and someone King Richard needs to keep on his side."

"I'm assuming you don't end up a feared member of the nobility by being an idiot. Assuming the demon king is the kind of threat everyone seems to think he is, then politics needs to go by the wayside in favor of survival. If he's not that big of a threat, what the hell am I doing here?"

Lyra blew out a breath and once again looked all of her fifteen hundred years. "The demon king is absolutely that big of a threat and you're completely right about what we need to do. The problem is, the hero has always defeated the demon king. That gives the nobility confidence you'll do the same. Their confidence has them jockeying for position and power during the inevitable rebuilding. I've seen it happen six times before and there's not a damn thing either of us can do about it."

"Swell. What about sparring?"

"I'll spar with you. I should've done that in the first place, but the previous heroes all had issues when it came to fighting women. Some ludicrous notions of chivalry. As if a woman with a sword wouldn't gut them every bit as quickly as a man if they faced each other on the battlefield."

Danny knew that all too well. He'd seen plenty of female insurgents. They could squeeze a rifle trigger as well as a man and in some cases better.

"I harbor no such illusions, ma'am. If we can move this training along, I'm ready when you are."

She smiled and drew her sword, a very sharp-looking steel sword. A dull-yellow glow surrounded the blade. "I like your attitude. I had my doubts in the throne room after you arrived, but you're clearly more sensible than the other heroes I've trained."

Danny had his helmet halfway back on then paused. "What do you mean?"

"I mean they had these lofty ideas about what being the hero meant. They thought they were some sort of noble avenger or something, here to make the world a better, more honorable place. They were sweet ideas, and I wish they were the truth, but in reality the hero is a warrior summoned to kill our enemy. There's nothing especially honorable about bringing a child here to fight your battles for you. I was relieved when you said you were an adult."

"I'm glad one of us is relieved. As for me, now that I've had a couple days to think about things, I figure the demon king is coming one way or another and even if I wanted to walk away, I suspect trouble will come calling wherever I go. That being the case, best to stay where I have a teacher and an army to fight with." He plonked the helmet in place and cinched the chin strap down. "Now let's do this."

# CHAPTER 8

Danny trudged through the castle halls back to his room. He'd been sore plenty of times during basic, but tonight might take the cake. He'd sparred with Lyra for ten hours before she took pity on him and called it a day. She'd barely been breathing hard at the end while Danny sounded like an asthmatic ninety-year-old. He wished he felt that good.

On the plus side, the memories had stopped popping up at random and his swordplay was now smooth and effortless. Getting used to these skills—not learning them, his host had already done that for him—was among the stranger things he'd ever done. None of it seemed possible. Though he'd certainly heard of muscle memory, this was another level.

Despite living his entire life on a world where magic was both well-known and not especially rare, Danny had very limited experience dealing with it. In basic they were taught to avoid weaponized humans, as the military called wizards, at all costs. Mostly the only wizards he knew were the handful the military kept around to heal wounded soldiers.

Having magic of his own, the power and responsibility, was a lot and he hadn't started properly training yet. That would, in fact, begin the day after tomorrow. First Lyra wanted to thrash him some more in the sparring ring.

When his room came into view Danny slumped with relief, or he did for the two seconds it took him to notice Eve standing in front of his door. She offered a bright smile as she smoothed her white robes. "I wanted to check in and see how you were doing. Do you mind if we chat for a bit?"

He swallowed a disagreeable reply and nodded. If she'd come all this way, it wouldn't hurt to talk for a few minutes. He pushed the door open and Eve followed him in.

"You're looking a bit rough," she said.

"Ten hours of sparring with Lyra will do that to you."

She touched his back and warmth flooded in, taking away the pain. "Better?"

"Much, thank you." He dropped onto the bed and nodded toward his room's sole chair. "Have a seat."

She gathered her robe around her and settled down. "Thank you. I take it Lady Shael isn't going easy on you."

"She tried to set me up with some rookie knights as sparring partners but their asshole of a commander screwed it up. When I told him off, he took his people and left. No great loss given his attitude, but then my only option for a sparring partner was Lyra. Such a skinny woman shouldn't be able to hit so hard."

"Would that be Commander Morel?" Eve asked.

"Yup, that would be him. He wants to take over my training so he can score political points he thinks will improve his position after the war. Surviving the war strikes me as the more pressing priority, but then again I'm not a politician."

"Unfortunately, you sort of are."

Danny cocked his head. "Say what?"

"As the hero, you have a lot of sway over things. Your absolute necessity ensures that you can do basically whatever you want and no one will dare stop you. That makes you a wild card the nobles can't control. Normally that would put you in danger of ending up in a shallow grave or at the bottom of a peat bog. But they also know they can't beat the demon king without you. So, wild card."

Danny had said basically the same thing to Alban but hearing it repeated back to him in the context of politics surprised him.

"Okay, I'm open to advice. Other than focusing on my training, what should I do to avoid trouble? Assuming I win, I figure I've got around sixty or so years on this world. I'd prefer not to spend all those years dodging assassins."

"That's a difficult question, especially if you've already offended the Morel family. They're the sorts to hold a grudge." She offered a somewhat pained smile. "I fear I'm not the best person to help you with political matters. I've been locked up in the cathedral preparing for your summoning since I was ten. Court matters were well outside my area of instruction. But if you'd like to know more about the tenets of Adonael's faith, I can tell you all about them."

Danny would rather get poked with a sharp stick than hear about Adonael's faith. "What about the other kingdoms? Someone mentioned a meeting in the near future with some neighboring kings and other big shots. Can you tell me about them?"

Eve brightened. "Sure I can. The Five Kingdoms feature

prominently in the history of Adonael's faith. You see, this land was chosen to serve as the site of a great battle between good and evil. If we win, this world gets a five-thousand-year reprieve from the ravages of the demon lords."

"And if you lose?" Danny asked.

"Then Heaven will turn away from us and for five thousand years the angels will deny our calls for help. No divine magic and no summoning holy spirits to fight at our sides."

"That's quite a bet."

"Yes, but Adonael was clever. She found a loophole in the wager which allowed us to summon a powerful champion to lead us to victory."

"The heroes."

Eve nodded. "You are the hope of not only this world, but of Heaven itself. It's a great honor."

"If you say so. It seems to me you were looking for a way to ensure your victory and you didn't care what you had to do to win."

"That's a very negative way to look at it, but not completely wrong, especially from your point of view."

Danny really didn't want to have this discussion. It would piss him off all over again. "Forget that for now and tell me about the kingdoms themselves."

"Right. You see, the Five Kingdoms used to be one big kingdom. Due to internal strife, they broke up into five smaller kingdoms ruled by related monarchs, originally brothers but now distant cousins."

Danny was sure he'd heard something similar back on Earth. "Let me guess, the father died and the brothers got to fighting over the kingdom and in the end they decided to divide the country up to preserve the peace."

"Close. The king at the time knew his sons hated each

other and that whichever one he chose as his heir would be opposed by the other four. So he divided the kingdom himself before his death, giving each one a nation to rule with its size based on how much noble support the prince held. Villipan is the largest. Since it's also the home of the Crystal Cathedral, it wields the most influence in the modern era."

"How do the monarchs get along now?"

"Reasonably well considering they have to fight as a group to have any chance of defeating the demon king's army. If we manage to defeat all nine demon kings and in so doing eliminate the threat, I fear it won't be long before war breaks out between the kingdoms."

Danny yawned. "Sounds about right. Either way, I'll be long dead before it's an issue. I don't want to be rude, but I've got another early day tomorrow, so I think I'm going to call it a night."

Eve scrambled to her feet. "Of course, I didn't mean to keep you."

"You didn't. And thanks for the info, it was interesting."

Her face nearly glowed when she smiled. "If you like I can stop by every evening for a chat before you go to sleep."

"That would be nice." Especially since it would come with free magical healing.

"See you tomorrow then!" She skipped to the door and slipped out.

What an odd girl. On the plus side, unlike some of the people he'd met, Eve seemed like a solid person. Heaven knew he could use more of those in his life.

⏻

King Richard wanted few things less than he wanted to listen to Alban Morel. The subject of the conversation didn't matter. The mere fact that Alban was speaking acted like spikes into his brain. The knight commander had requested a meeting and, given who his brother was, Richard had been forced to grant it rather than tell him to go swimming in full armor, which was what he wanted to say when the request arrived.

And so he found himself seated in the private meeting room a little ways off the throne room listening to the arrogant fool rant and rave about being disrespected by Lyra and the new hero. Any moment now Richard expected flecks of spittle to start flying. Such lack of control was truly unbecoming of a kingdom noble, though, where Alban was concerned, rank and actual nobility of character were two very different things.

When Alban finally paused to catch his breath Richard said, "Let me see if I understand you correctly. You intentionally ignored Lyra's request for a light sparring match in order to make her look bad and when she called you out on it, you got pissy and took your knights back to the barracks, potentially retarding the growth of the only person capable of defeating the demon king and in so doing securing Villipan's continued existence. Have I missed anything?"

"I...no. It sounds so much worse when you say it like that. I was the one wronged here. The so-called hero has no discipline. His skills are unrefined and he doesn't know how to speak to his betters. Give him to me and I'll see that he's properly educated, with the lash if necessary."

Richard turned his gaze to the ceiling and prayed to Adonael for patience. This ignoramus must be some sort of divine test. As if the demon king wasn't bad enough.

"Alban, the hero has been here for three days. Do you truly expect him to be a master of swordsmanship and courtly manners in that length of time? And what is it with both you and my son thinking any sentence that includes both the hero and the lash should ever be spoken? I told Florian this and I'll tell you, Daniel is our one and only hope of victory. If you do anything to turn him further against us, so help me, brother of the duke or not, I'll have you stripped naked, covered in honey, and staked to an ant hill. Your petty ego means far less to me than the army of demons and monsters I have no doubt is headed this way as we speak. Do I make myself clear?"

Alban stared at him with a blank expression so amusing it took all of Richard's self-control not to laugh. Clearly this wasn't the reaction he'd been expecting. That fact spoke volumes about his stupidity as well as his arrogance.

"How dare you speak to a son of the Morel family in such a tone!"

Richard leapt to his feet. He'd had all he could take. "I am Richard de Villipan, king of this nation, and I will speak to you in any way I choose. If you wish to whine to your brother about it, then do so. I doubt he has any more interest in your stupidity than I do. Now take yourself from my sight before I do something we'll both regret."

Alban turned on his heel and walked out, back rigid and fists clenched. He would cause more trouble before this was over, Richard had no doubt. But that was a problem for another day. Right now, he needed a drink.

"You let your temper get the best of you again." His lovely wife emerged from the shadows where she'd been watching the conversation, two glasses of red wine in her hands.

Richard accepted a glass and took a long drink. "That

nitwit brings out the worst in me, Cecile. I got a report from the scouts this morning. They spotted packs of hellhounds prowling the edge of Fell Forest. The demons stared right at them and let them go. The damn monsters want us to know they're here and can attack at any time."

"You should send Alban and his knights to deal with them. Tell him he can claim all the glory for the first victory."

Robert dropped back into his chair and sighed. "If I could send him by himself, I would happily do so. The knights, unfortunately, I need to hold back until we face their main army. Despite their useless leader, they are good men. I'll not throw their lives away, even if I could rid myself of Alban in the process."

"Perhaps if he continues to push her, Lyra will rid you of the man."

"I should be so lucky. No, she'll do nothing to put her people in danger. Killing a kingdom noble, including a useless one, definitely falls into that category. Unfortunately, I fear we're stuck with dear Alban for the rest of his hopefully short natural life."

Cecile kissed the top of his head. "Heavy is the crown, dear. Now, let's go to bed. I understand the hero gets started early and you don't want to miss his first attempt at magic tomorrow."

"I was thinking of waiting until he'd established a bit of control before going to watch."

"Afraid he might blow you to smithereens?"

"The thought had crossed my mind. The only good thing about getting blown up is that I wouldn't have to deal with Alban anymore. Though I shudder to think what might come of Villipan with him and Florian both having authority."

"Florian's a clever boy," Cecile said, her tone a fraction sharp. She did dote on her darling son.

"In some respects, yes. His main problem is an excess of pride."

"Were you less proud at Florian's age?" she countered.

"No, I might well have been worse. All princes are. That's why you don't want them becoming kings until they're older. I'll be skipping magic practice tomorrow."

Cecile only smiled, but he had a fair idea what she was thinking. Richard didn't care if she thought him a coward. A dead king was no use to anyone.

# CHAPTER 9

Danny walked beside Lyra down the streets of the aptly named Villipan City. They wore hooded cloaks and the people out and about this early paid them no attention. The workers clearly had more pressing things to concern themselves with than a pair of strangers minding their own business.

It felt strange being outside without minders. Albert and Jean had been his shadows for basically as long as he'd been here. Still, this was Danny's first trip outside the castle since Eve introduced him to the king and he planned to enjoy it. At least as much as he could knowing his first attempt at using magic waited at the end of their walk. When he thought about unleashing the fire, it terrified him. He felt like a toddler someone had given a flamethrower. There was no way it could end well.

He took a deep breath of cool morning air and caught a whiff of baking bread. Though full after a breakfast of hash with the guards, he still found the smell tantalizing. For some reason they didn't serve bread in the dining hall he used. Maybe they didn't serve it in the castle at all. He didn't know. Danny found himself smiling at the idea that the king might have a gluten sensitivity.

His amusement was cut short by a shout, a crash and a scream from their right. Lyra moved to put herself between him and whatever was causing the ruckus. That stung his pride, but having seen her fight, Danny harbored no illusions about which of them was better suited to dealing with a potential threat. For the time being, that was.

"What's going on?" Danny asked.

"I don't know, but it's coming from the direction of the Adventurers Guild so you can be sure they're the problem. Undisciplined amateurs, the lot of them. Still, they're not totally useless, especially when the problem is too small for the army and too big for a village militia. I just wish they weren't drunk all the time."

"Sometimes when you put your life on the line, you need to blow off steam when you return to base. As long as they're not breaking anything other than noise ordinances it seems like a minor deal."

Lyra finally relaxed when it became clear there was no immediate threat and they set out again. Nothing else troubled them and fifteen minutes after leaving the castle, they passed through the final city gate and onto a dirt road that ran generally west for as far as Danny could see.

"Where to now?" he asked.

"An empty field on Crown property. It's generally used for large-scale training exercises, but will suit our needs perfectly."

Danny nodded and followed her when she turned off the

road and started across a field dotted with wildflowers. It was yet another beautiful sight. While he dearly missed Wi-Fi and endless movies, the natural beauty of this world almost made up for it. He wished there was some way he could show it to Suzy, but that was impossible. He'd been trying his best not to think about her, but sometimes that hurt worse than the memories.

The hike to reach their practice grounds took longer than the walk through the city. But finally, they reached a field that looked like it had either been recently grazed by very thorough sheep or someone had run a lawn mower over it.

Lyra took down the hood of her cloak and turned to face him, her golden eyes glowing a bit brighter than usual. "It's time to begin your magical training. As with the sword, all the knowledge you need is already locked up in your mind. Each spell will trigger memories and the knowledge will be yours to use as you wish. Before we begin casting proper spells, I want to confirm that your magic is as strong as I first thought."

Danny didn't like the sound of that. "Okay, but are you sure it's safe?"

"There's no better place to test it. The nearest civilization is miles away. The worst you can do is burn some grass and smash a few trees."

"Okay." She was the instructor; if this was what she wanted, he'd do his best. "What should I do?"

"Instead of drawing the ether into your body, picture it gathering in your hand. Make it into a ball of energy. Keep adding to the ball until it feels like it's about to break apart. That's the sign you've reached your maximum. As soon as you feel it, hurl the gathered energy into the center of the clearing while picturing it exploding."

Sounded simple enough. Danny held out his right hand and pictured the fire gathering there. The magic responded at once and it grew larger by the moment.

"Keep it compressed," Lyra said. "No bigger than an apple. The denser the energy, the bigger the blast."

Right, okay. Basically he was making a magic hand grenade. As soon as the image of what he wanted solidified, the magic rushed in even faster. He kept the image firmly in mind as more and more power gathered above his hand.

Danny wasn't sure how much more he should do, but the power remained completely stable, so he kept going. He lost all track of time as he worked, but at last, at the very edge of his awareness, he felt a faint ripple in the fabric of the spell.

Taking that as a signal, he threw his magic grenade into the center of the clearing.

The explosion didn't disappoint. A massive fireball erupted, filling a third of the field with blueish white flames that roared and billowed up into the sky. When they finally vanished, only a circle of charred earth remained.

"How'd I do?" Danny asked.

Lyra looked a bit paler than usual, but she nodded and said, "More than adequate. Focusing on control will once again be our primary goal. Do you need to rest before we begin some basic spellcasting?"

"No, I'm fine. Please begin whenever you're ready."

"Of course you're fine," she muttered so softly he barely heard it. "Alright, we'll start with some defensive magic."

So saying, they got to work. Danny created shields, armor, walls, energy barriers designed to stop particular elemental attacks. With each spell, his mind was assaulted by memories. That was the worst part. Casting the spells themselves took almost nothing out of him, but dealing with

JAMES E. WISHER

the foreign memories gradually brought on a blazing headache.

"Enough. I feel like my head's going to burst. How many spells did this guy know?"

Lyra frowned. "I'm not sure exactly, though since he won the contest to become your host, I'd think over a hundred."

Danny withered inside. "A hundred? My brain's going to melt. How many did we do today?"

"Ten. Don't worry, your brain isn't going to melt. The spells are burned into the host brain, it's your soul that's having trouble dealing with them. It recognizes the memories as not part of you and is trying to stop them. The conflict between your soul and your host body is what causes the headaches and nightmares. All the heroes go through this process. The faster you work through all his knowledge, the faster it'll be over."

"Yeah, I understand that, but after a certain point the pain gets so bad I can't concentrate anymore."

"Then that's where we stop and switch to something else. In this case, unarmed combat."

"Come again?"

"Learning unarmed combat is important if you ever lose your weapon in battle. It can be the difference between life and death."

"I'm not complaining. I got my black belt certification in the Marine Corps Martial Arts Program three months before you brought me here. This is something I should be able to do without any memories getting in the way."

Lyra set her sword on the ground and lowered her stance. "Show me. And no magic."

Danny obliged and for the next hour they threw punches and kicks, wrestled and did groundwork. It was a relief to use his own training instead of relying on what he considered stolen skills. At last they separated, both of them out of breath for a change.

"Enough," Lyra said. "I think your unarmed combat skills are better than all the other heroes combined. It's easy to see that you've used them in a real fight. In one chokehold in particular I could tell you could've broken my neck had you wished to."

Danny nodded. "One of the focuses of our training is learning how much force to use in any given situation."

"How's your headache?"

"Gone." He chuckled. "It goes away quickly once I stop thinking."

"Want to practice a couple more spells before we go back?" It came as a surprise when she didn't give him an order.

In truth, the last thing Danny wanted was to practice more spells, but the sooner he got through them, the sooner he'd be free of the memory attacks, as he'd come to think of them. "Sure, though I don't know how long I'll last."

The answer was five more spells. After the fifth one his headache came roaring back, twice as bad as before. If there was ever a sign they needed to quit, that was it.

"You did well today," Lyra said. "We'll alternate between combat and magic training from now on. I'd say two, maybe three weeks and you'll have all your memories integrated."

That sounded excellent to Danny. Right now, he'd happily pay an executioner to cut his head off just to end the pain.

Eve leaned against the wall outside Daniel's room. One of the servants, a devout follower of Adonael, had brought her word that he'd arrived at the dining hall. Apparently he hadn't been looking too good. Not a surprise since Lady Shael had a reputation as a difficult instructor. Though the results spoke for themselves: six heroes trained and six demon kings defeated.

If she couldn't help with Daniel's combat training, she was determined to educate him on practical matters. He'd seemed to appreciate her magical healing last time as well. If it helped, she was happy to offer another casting. It was her duty as his chosen companion.

"This is a surprise." Eve looked to her right and found Princess Claudette approaching. She was wearing a rather scandalous red dress that exposed a great deal of cleavage. "I didn't expect to find another woman waiting outside the hero's room. Do I have competition for his affection?"

Eve knew the rumors about Claudette and her cheeks warmed when she thought about them. "I'm giving him lessons on history and geography as well as healing any sore or strained muscles he might have after training."

"And nothing else? Your loss, I suppose. Could you skip tonight? I'm hoping to see if he's fully functional now." Claudette offered a suggestive waggle of her eyebrows.

"After a day of training, I'm sure he won't be interested in anything too physically demanding. And I can handle any injuries better than you."

"My dear Eve, I assure you no man has ever been so tired that he wouldn't perk up at my arrival. Assuming he still has a pulse, *I'm* sure he'll want to see me more than you. Now run along. I'll even send a servant to let you know when we're finished, though I doubt he'll be interested in any history lessons."

Eve bristled at the princess's tone. "Now see here. Daniel's lessons are more important than... that sort of thing. He needs to be ready for the Kings' Conclave."

"The other kings don't care about his manners, only that he's strong enough to do what he has to. I'll be the one to keep him properly motivated."

The two women glared at each other. Eve wouldn't give in on this. She had her duty to both Adonael and Daniel. And she refused to let some self-centered princess keep her from doing it.

"Eve? Princess?" They'd been so focused on each other, neither woman had noticed Daniel approaching from the opposite direction. "I didn't expect to find both of you here. It's been a long day and I fear I'm in no fit shape for company. If you'll both excuse me, I'm going to turn in early."

Claudette spun in a swirl of blond hair to face Daniel. "Are you sure? I could help you relax. Release some pressure, as it were."

"Some magical healing might help," Eve said.

Daniel's pained expression deepened. "I've been getting hammered with memory headaches today. My body is fine, but my mind is exhausted. I need to sleep. Alone. If you ladies will excuse me..."

He brushed past them, slipped into his room, and closed the door firmly. Eve caught the faint click of the bolt sliding into place.

"He turned me down," Claudette said. "No one has ever turned me down before."

She looked down at herself, plumped her breasts up a bit,

not that they needed any plumping, and turned to Eve. "There's nothing wrong with me, is there?"

Eve might be considered naïve by some, but she knew a loaded question when she heard one. "Not at all, Princess. I think you just have bad timing. I guess we both do tonight. I'm going to return to the cathedral. Good evening."

She offered a polite bow and hurried away, a faint smile curving her lips. She didn't win that round, but she didn't lose either.

# CHAPTER 10

D anny sat in the dust of the training yard and took slow, deep breaths. Mixing magical control with combat took a lot out of him. He could only maintain full power for about five minutes before he needed to rest.

Ten days had passed since Danny's arrival on Valindor and he'd settled into a routine, alternating days of magic and combat training combined with evading Princess Claudette, which he considered a form of stealth training. Why she was so obsessed with him, Danny couldn't say. When he'd asked Albert about it all he got was a nervous cough and a refusal to meet his gaze. Eve hadn't been much more forthcoming, simply stating the princess had certain appetites and had been that way since she became an adult.

Sounded like she was hornier than average, no harm in that. Claudette was hot enough to have any man she wanted. Danny had mostly made peace with the fact that he was living a new life and Earth Danny was dead. When he thought about it through that lens, it wouldn't be cheating on

Suzy if he slept with Claudette. He was never going to see her again. Moving on with his new life wasn't optional, it was necessary.

At least those were the excuses he gave himself. It still felt wrong and definitely too soon. He also hadn't heard anyone talk about birth control. Knocking up the princess then getting himself killed and not being there for his kid didn't sit right with Danny. There were certain responsibilities you couldn't walk away from and taking care of your kid was the most important of them.

And so he evaded when he could and made excuses when he couldn't. He had to give Claudette credit; she wasn't easily discouraged.

"Ready for another round?" Lyra asked. His instructor had vastly more stamina when it came to body strengthening magic.

Danny forced himself to his feet. "Sure. Quick question. Is birth control a thing on this world?"

Lyra stared at him for a moment. "Why?"

Danny explained about the princess. "I don't want any accidents."

"There are potions women can take that will purge an unwanted child, but there's nothing I know of that can safely prevent pregnancy."

"That's what I was afraid of. Guess I'll have to keep avoiding her. Thanks for the info."

Danny took up his wooden sword and called the fire into his body. The response was instantaneous. His skin became as hard as steel and his bones unbreakable. His sense of pain dulled to nothing. It was like the magic turned him into a war machine.

Lyra came at him. Their swords sounded like machine

guns they hit so fast.

Danny forced her back. She might have better stamina, but while he could use his power, he was stronger and faster than her. After thirty seconds Lyra's sword went flying.

He released the magic and stepped back. "How was that?"

"Perfect if the goal is victory."

Not the answer he expected. "Is that not the goal?"

"From now on it isn't. We've established that you can beat me in a sword fight anytime you want. The new goal is to make the fights last as long as possible to extend your maximum combat time. The third hero was the best at this. He could fight at full strength for an hour. That's fifteen minutes longer than me. Unfortunately, he wasn't anywhere near as strong as you. Given the amount of ether you're channeling, half an hour is a good target. If you can't win a fight in that length of time, you should run."

Danny barked a laugh. "I guess that's an option for any fight save the last one. Speaking of, no one's told me anything about the enemy army. I haven't seen the king since that day in the throne room. Where are they now?"

"Fighting's picked up at the border. Probing attacks have struck all along the north and west edges of Fell Forest. So far nothing the regular army can't handle. As for King Richard, he's constantly busy with the generals. I'm sure I can arrange a meeting if you'd like one."

Danny had no desire to meet with the king if he didn't have to. "No, that's fine. I was just curious. I'm surprised regular soldiers are doing so well against magical threats."

"Have you noticed there are no wizards in the city?" Lyra asked.

"I hadn't thought anything of it, but now that you

mention it, I am surprised there isn't a royal wizard protecting the king or something."

"The reason they're absent is that every wizard the Five Kingdoms can deploy is with the army enchanting their weapons. The priests of Branik and the Binder in Chains are there as well, along with followers of the Goddess, Lady of Healing, taking care of the wounded. You and I, along with a handful of Adonael's priests, are the only magic users not on the border."

"What about the adventurers?"

Lyra's face twisted with distaste. "Adventurers aren't aligned with any nation. If the city's attacked, they'll fight to protect themselves. Some of them will take contracts to fight in the war, but most prefer smaller-scale combat. When it's over, they'll be making a fortune hunting down stray demons and monsters."

"On the plus side, that will mean I defeated the demon king. Speaking of, does anyone know where the guy is?"

"Most likely in the Castle of the Demon King at the heart of Fell Forest. That's where the final battle always takes place."

"Why is there a castle of the demon king?" Danny wanted to laugh at the absurdity of it, but Lyra sounded dead serious. "Seems like the sort of thing you should tear down after the war."

"Usually it's mostly torn down during the battle between the hero and the demon king. The problem is, there's a hell gate under the castle that can't be sealed until the final demon king is defeated. The magic of the hell gate rebuilds the castle over and over so it's ready for the next demon king to consecrate to his patron. We can't station a force there to intercept the enemy since the corruption would kill any human who lingered for more than a day or two."

"That's pretty far from ideal. It's getting dark, do you want to go another round or call it a night?" Danny asked.

"Let's call it a night. We're going to the field tomorrow to practice elemental spells. That will no doubt unleash a number of memories for you to deal with. Being extra well rested can only help."

Danny wasn't about to argue. He handed Lyra his practice sword. "See you in the morning then."

With that he headed back for the castle with Jean silently following him. The guard still hadn't spoken more than a handful of words. Chatty, he definitely was not.

Dinner was the usual beef stew and watered wine. Though he knew he should sleep, Danny found his mind too busy. He was curious about the other heroes and how they lived their lives after the final battle. He couldn't be the only one that missed the conveniences of Earth. He'd swing by the library and see if they had anything about the previous heroes.

At the dining hall door he went the opposite way from his room. He'd barely taken a step when Jean said, "Where are you going, my lord? Your room is the other way."

"I know where my room is. I'm going to the library to find a book. I thought I might read myself to sleep tonight. It'll make a pleasant change of pace."

Jean looked slightly panicked and Danny wasn't sure why. He'd been a good sport about the constant training. Some of it was even fun. It wasn't like he was unfamiliar with training. They did a ton of it between deployments. But if he decided he wanted to read for a couple hours before bed, then damned if he wasn't going to do so.

He kept going with his now-reluctant shadow following along. He nodded to a couple of unfamiliar servants who stopped in the middle of the hall to stare at him. Danny hadn't visited this part of the castle since Eve showed him around his first day. He'd been so tired every night that the idea of more thinking caused him physical pain. He must be getting used to things now.

His excellent sense of direction served him well and he soon stood in front of the library door. It wasn't locked and he pushed it open without knocking. He'd been afraid they might close down at night, but some kind of magical light shone down on the scores of bookcases. The few scattered tables were empty, but a young woman stood behind the counter at the rear of the room.

Having no desire to search on his own, Danny marched right over to her. Blond haired, blue eyed, and pale, with a slender build, she looked like every other human Danny had met in Villipan. She wore a tan apron over a simple blue dress.

"Can I help you?" she asked.

"I'm looking for a book on the heroes. I thought it might help my training if I knew more about what they dealt with in the past."

Her eyes got very wide very quickly. "Sir Hero. Forgive me, I didn't recognize you."

"No reason you should've since we haven't been introduced. So can you help me out with the book?"

"Um, do you have permission?"

Danny frowned and the girl flinched like she feared he might hit her. "Why do I need permission to read a book?"

"The library is only for nobles. Not that most commoners can read anyway, but that's the rule."

Was that what had Jean so worked up? "That's not a problem. The hero is considered the same rank as the upper nobility and I'm giving myself permission. So, a book on the heroes?"

"Yes, my lord. The definitive work on the subject is the History of the Saviors of Valindor. We have the most recent edition. It was updated after the sixth hero defeated the demon king of that cycle. Wait here and I'll find it for you."

"Thank you."

She hustled out from behind her desk and disappeared into the stacks. Danny turned and found Jean outside the door practically trembling. He walked over. "Are you really worried I'm going to get into trouble for taking a book out of the library?"

"I'm less worried now that I know what your rank is considered. Still, best for commoners like me to stay out of noble business. I don't even like being in this part of the castle. Never know what sort of nobleman you might run into."

"Sounds like you'd prefer to be out in the field with the army."

Jean quickly shook his head in denial. "Not at all, sir. Nobles make me nervous but demons scare the hell out of me, pun intended."

Sounded like Danny didn't end up with the bravest guard in the history of the world.

"She's back," Jean said.

Danny quick-stepped over to the table and took a leather-bound tome from the librarian. "Thanks, I appreciate it."

"Not at all, sir. One request if I may." When Danny nodded she continued. "Please bring it back if you're planning to leave the castle for an extended period. I can't go into people's rooms looking for missing books."

Danny smiled. "You take your job seriously. I appreciate that. Don't worry, I'll be sure to bring it back as soon as I'm done."

"Thank you very much, my lord." She curtsied and lowered her gaze at the same time.

For some reason that triggered a memory which informed him of the correct etiquette for a commoner speaking to a noble. Useless, but at least he didn't get a headache to go with it.

Danny shook his head and tucked the book under his arm. When they passed the dining hall—as soon as they were back in commoner land—Jean let out a sigh of relief.

Just to tease him Danny said, "You know the princess might be outside my room again."

"Princess Claudette doesn't frighten me the way some nobles do. She has a more relaxed reputation."

"That's one way to describe it," Danny said.

Jean let out a squeak of laughter before stifling it.

"What about Eve? She doesn't bother you?"

"No, sir. Lady Carre was born common and elevated by Adonael's grace. She's one of us."

Danny hadn't heard that before. It explained why Eve was so easy to talk to.

In the end, neither the princess nor Eve were waiting outside his room today. He had no idea why that should be, but was glad all the same. The history of his predecessors had him curious. It was time to find out exactly what the prior heroes had done to earn the title.

# CHAPTER 11

After changing out of his sweat-stained clothes and washing up—man, what he wouldn't give for a proper shower—Danny settled in to read. He wasn't technically supposed to cast spells without supervision yet, but summoning a light should be safe enough. It was either that or read by candlelight, a prospect that didn't thrill him and would probably make the librarian nervous.

With his tiny glowing sphere in position, Danny opened the book. The first page was all about the author and his no-doubt-impressive credentials. Ignoring that, he moved on to the first hero, a fifteen-year-old boy named Toshiro. There were tales of battle and heroics, and a brief mention of romance with the princess at the time. Maybe there was a tradition to help explain Claudette's behavior. None of it was terribly interesting until he got to the part about the battle with the demon king. According to the author, the story was copied word for word from a document written by Toshiro himself.

*The sight of the dark castle left him shaking. It had a presence,* almost an awareness about it. The sheer malevolence radiating from the black stone seemed to be trying to crush his spirit. Taking those final steps alone was among the hardest things he had ever done.

And he had to face it alone. Only the one wearing the hero's armor was protected from the corruption that surrounded the castle. His worthy companions were forced to remain behind along with Shael Sensei. This was the hero's battle and he had to fight it by himself.

Toshiro strode through the dark halls, his sword gripped tight. His heart pounded such that he feared the enemy might hear him coming.

At last, in the heart of the castle, he found the demon king, a great burly brute of a man wrapped in black armor from head to toe and holding a battle ax sized for a giant. Behind him, the hell gate spewed corruption like a volcano shooting lava. Only the hero's mithril armor allowed Toshiro to remain on his feet. It was truly a gift from Heaven as Shael Sensei had told him.

No words were wasted before the first blow fell. The force of the demon king's attack sent Toshiro flying across the room to slam into the wall with bone-breaking force.

Once again his armor along with his skill using physical enhancement saved him.

Toshiro kicked off the wall, his mithril katana leading.

Back and forth they went, but at last the katana found a home in the demon king's heart. The monster collapsed and, just to be sure, Toshiro sliced his head off. The oppressive atmosphere quickly faded. He staggered his way out and in the courtyard found his companions and teacher waiting. Much rejoicing and many tears followed.

The battle was over; the day was theirs.

That confirmed Danny would have to fight the demon

king on his own. No one had shown him any special armor or sword. Figured it was a katana since the first hero was from the empire. Danny had never used one. He'd have to mention that to Lyra. He needed to spend some time getting used to it before his life depended on using the weapon.

What followed was a description of Toshiro's life after his victory. A mansion was built for him on the outskirts of Villipan City, servants were provided, and he even married the princess. Not a bad life all things considered. He died peacefully at the age of ninety-seven.

And not ten years later the second demon king appeared.

The second hero was summoned, this time a sixteen-year-old boy named Rengie. The details of his training were painfully familiar to Danny. His ending, unfortunately, was a good deal less happy than Toshiro's. Rengie died in battle with the demon king, though he did succeed in taking his foe with him. A statue was raised in his honor behind the Crystal Cathedral.

Danny skimmed a few more entries. The rest of the heroes had stories almost identical to Rengie's. None of them survived the battle with the demon king and each got a statue in his honor. Only one out of six survived his final battle. Not the best odds.

The rest of the book was historical details and a ton of conjecture by the author about how brave the heroes were to give their lives for the people. Danny doubted any of them went into their fight expecting to give their lives for the people. He certainly had no intention of dying here if he could help it. In fact, part of him was seriously contemplating ditching this hero thing and starting over somewhere else. Only his confidence that, should the demon king not be defeated, there wouldn't be anywhere safe to go kept him from ditching this place for greener pastures.

When Danny finally let his light fade, sleep was a long time coming.

○

The next day was a magic-learning day and after breakfast Danny and Lyra set out for the training grounds. Danny was exhausted after a miserable night contemplating his seemingly likely death at the hand of the current demon king. Across from him, Lyra had her narrow face twisted up in a grimace. That was unusual. From all he'd seen, she usually kept her emotions well under control.

Halfway through the city Danny said, "I want to make a side trip this morning."

Lyra turned her face his way. The top half was shaded by her hood so only her chin and glowing eyes were visible. "What sort of side trip?"

"I want to see the hero's mansion. If by some miracle I survive, I want to know where I'll be living."

"Sounds like Eve's been talking about your predecessors."

"No, she never mentioned them. Though she is oddly obsessed with which fork I should use for which dish at the gala. I got a history book from the library last night. A little reading before bed struck me as a good idea. Apparently no one thought it was important to tell me five out of the six previous heroes died in the final battle. Kind of an important bit of information."

"You're mistaken. What's important is that they all defeated their demon king, as I'm confident you will."

Danny stopped in his tracks. "Easy for you to say. What are a few dead humans to an immortal elf? It's no skin off your bony ass if I die as long as you can get back to your normal life. I, on the other hand, take the possibility of my death very seriously."

"So what do you want to do about it? Run away? If you went far enough, fast enough, you might put enough distance between yourself and Villipan that you could live out your life in peace before results of your failure reached you. The fact that you'd be condemning hundreds of thousands to death or slavery in the process isn't a big deal. This isn't even your world. Right?"

"I thought about that last night. After I read the heroes' history, I stared into the dark and wondered. What do I owe you? What do I owe this world? I could only come up with one answer: nothing. I owe this world nothing. Everything you've done is wrong as far as I'm concerned. Dragging innocent people into your war against their will is cruel. It would serve you all right if I left."

"I can't allow that," Lyra said. "Everything you said is correct, but in the end, our need hasn't changed. Only you can defeat the demon king."

Danny bristled at the implication of her statement. "You can't allow it? Do you think you can force me to fight if I choose not to? Do you have a prison that can hold me should I wish to leave? Perhaps when I reach the castle, I'll offer to serve the demon king. How do you imagine that would go?"

"You're right. I can't force you to fight and we have no prison capable of holding you. And suppose we did, without the proper training, you'd have no hope of winning anyway. As for serving the demon king, that wouldn't go well for you. You have Adonael's blessing. No one serving the demon lords would ever team up with you."

"Hey!" shouted the driver of a heavily laden merchant wagon. "Get the hell out of the road, you're blocking traffic."

They slipped to the side and the wagon clattered on.

"So what will you do?" She sounded beyond weary.

"Show me the mansion. Show me something to convince me the risk is worth it. I've already died once. I don't want to do it again. The odds terrify me."

"Would it help if I told you that you really are the strongest hero to date?"

"Since I know little about the heroes and nothing about the demon king, that doesn't help in the least."

"Fine. I'll take you to the mansion. It's on a beautiful estate. If you live, I'll move out and take my granddaughters with me."

Danny sighed. "No need for that. I always liked kids. You're all welcome to stay."

She shot him a look. "I thought you hated elf-bloods."

"So did I, but you don't seem so bad despite your blood. Maybe we already killed all the bad ones when they invaded."

"You have an odd way of giving compliments."

They set out again, this time on a different path through the city. They passed through busy residential areas until finally reaching the north gate. Less than half a mile down the road Lyra turned up a dirt path that led to a sprawling mansion surrounded by manicured grounds. Trees jutted up behind it, but he couldn't tell how far away they were.

"Wow. They knew how to properly thank the first hero, no doubt about it. How did you end up living here?"

"Wasn't my idea. When the second hero died, the king at the time asked me to move in. He feared squatters setting up camp if it remained empty. We only use five rooms, though the girls do enjoy playing hide and seek in the rest of the house."

If the mansion had less than thirty rooms, Danny would eat his boots. "You must have staff to keep up the grounds."

"A group of elf-blood survivors stops by once a week and uses their earth magic to keep the grounds properly groomed. I pay them a small stipend which helps the settlement."

Beyond the garden, three steps led up to the front porch. Lyra went right in without knocking. The entry hall was bigger than Danny's suite in the castle. The furniture was covered with cloths to protect it from dust and the whole place gave off a haunted-castle vibe. Assuming he survived, Danny wasn't sure he'd want to live there.

"Grandma!" Two little girls came barreling into the hall. They wore white dresses and their long dark hair streamed behind them as they ran. And that was all he saw before they practically tackled Lyra.

She hugged them both and Danny could barely suppress a warm smile at the scene.

At last Lyra said, "Girls, I'd like to introduce you to someone. This is Daniel, the new hero."

Two little faces peeked at him from behind Lyra's legs. Their almond-shaped eyes were dark and didn't glow. That golden light must be something unique to Lyra rather than an elf thing.

"Hello there." Danny waved. "It's nice to meet you both."

After a moment of staring one of them inched her way out from behind Lyra. "I'm Tara. That's Nora. She's a scaredy cat."

Nora stomped indignantly out from behind Lyra. "I am

not. Grandma always says we should be careful around humans."

"Not humans she brings home with her, dummy."

"I'm not a dummy!" Nora stomped her foot.

"Come on, girls," Danny said. "No fighting. Sisters should look out for each other, not argue."

"Do you have a sister?" Nora asked.

Danny sat on the floor so he wouldn't be towering over them. "No, though I do have a little brother. He turned eighteen a couple months ago."

"Eighteen!" Nora said. "He's still a baby."

Tara gave a shake of her head. "Told you she was a dummy. Humans don't age like we do. For a human, eighteen is all grown up. Right, Grandma?"

Lyra was looking down at them with the softest, most gentle expression he'd seen on her face so far. "That's right, dearheart. Their souls burn bright, but not for long."

"How come?" Tara asked.

Nora's hand shot up. "I know, I know. It's because they don't have the blood of Heaven in them like we do, right?"

"Exactly." Lyra folded her long legs under her and sat facing Danny. "Our ancient ancestors came to this world from Heaven at the bidding of the archangels. The reasons are lost to time, but we know when they left, a number of half-elves had been born. And from them, all other elf-bloods are descended."

Nora stuck her tongue out at Tara and Danny couldn't hold in a laugh. He and Lyra hung around the mansion for hours. He played hide and seek with the girls, they had lunch together—a rare treat for him—and in the afternoon they showed him the woods behind the house.

It was a wonderful break from training and Danny had

needed it worse than he thought, especially after reading about the heroes. An hour before sunset they said their goodbyes, but Danny promised to visit them again which brought a cheer.

As he and Lyra walked away from the mansion Danny said, "They're sweet kids. Is it okay to leave them here alone?"

"The mansion is warded. Anyone trying to enter when I'm not present will regret it." She blew out a long breath. "You were very good with them. The girls haven't had that much fun in far too long."

"Whenever my team went into a village, I was in charge of playing with the kids. I had a knack with them. It's also amazing what kids will blurt out without thinking. I got a lot of intel that way."

"I have to apologize for snapping at you earlier. I had just gotten word of the first major incursion by enemy forces. The scout force that spotted them took major casualties, including an elf-blood ranger, and the knights who defeated the demons lost people as well. The loss of even one of my people hurts, especially given how few of us there are. Try as I might to convince them otherwise, there are a few brave souls that refuse to remain safe in the settlement." She gave a weary shake of her head. "I thought we'd have more time, but if things have advanced this far already, we need to accelerate your training."

"I was in a bad mood as well. Let's chalk it up to stress and move forward. As for the training, I don't know how much more I can do on any given day."

"We'll be going out on combat missions to give you a taste of real fighting. Not every day—there's still plenty you need to learn—but at minimum once or twice a month, assuming we have a month. I take it that means you've decided to fight rather than run?"

"I think I had already decided. I admit to some doubts when I learned the odds of surviving, but seeing your granddaughters reaffirmed my commitment. One way or the other, I'm going to kill the demon king. What are we doing tomorrow?"

"Tomorrow, I'll show you the hero's sword and armor."

In the war room at the heart of Villipan Castle, King Richard studied a map of the Five Kingdoms. The first major attack happened in the northwest, only a couple miles from the first monster encounter. It seemed that the demon king was planning a major push from that direction. Or so all the generals thought.

Richard had his doubts. He'd studied the military histories the same way every nobleman did. The demon kings were all about raw power and aggression. None of them had shown the least bit of subtlety in any of their attacks. Nevertheless, something seemed off to him. There was unsubtle and then there was stupid.

Such a small attack would only serve to draw their attention north. If that was truly where the primary invasion was going to happen, the demons should've made their raid somewhere else to serve as a distraction and divide the kingdom's forces.

That's what Richard would've done in their place. Perhaps he was overthinking things. When you had demons, undead, and all sorts of other monsters at your command, concentrating your enemies in one place so you could crush them in one go made a certain amount of sense.

Whatever the case, the army wasn't big enough to cover every avenue of attack. He'd have to trust that he wasn't being tricked and hope for the best.

The door squeaked as it opened and he looked up to find Lyra standing there. He always found her glowing eyes unsettling.

"Well?"

"He's committed. I took him to see the hero's mansion, but it was the girls who really convinced him. Daniel will see the fight through, I'm sure of it."

Richard blew out a breath. Counting on the hero was always a risky proposition. He'd hoped that Claudette would be able to reinforce his determination, but she claimed he showed no interest in being with her. According to her, Daniel was more interested in spending his evenings with Eve. Her annoyance had been amusing mainly for its pettiness.

"Who'd have thought two kids would be more effective than my daughter? Do you think he prefers men? I could make arrangements."

Lyra joined him beside the map table. "No, he's interested in Princess Claudette. He asked me about ways to prevent pregnancy, so he's definitely thinking about her. The problem is, he's worried about leaving an orphan behind should he be killed in the fighting. An honorable thought that surprised me."

"Really? That is surprising. Surely he knows any child would be well cared for. The offspring of a royal princess and the hero would certainly turn out to be a valuable addition to our bloodline."

"He's more worried about a child of his growing up without a father. He said it would be irresponsible to bring a baby into the world if you weren't going to be around to raise it."

"Claudette will be relieved. She had begun to fear her feminine charms were losing their power. What's the plan for his training? This most recent attack makes me think the timeline might be advancing faster than we anticipated."

"Tomorrow he'll practice in the hero's armor for the first time. He's three-quarters done with spell training. We should finish that this week. Once his mind is free from stray memories, I plan to take him into the field for live combat."

"The other kings will be bringing their champions to the gala. They'll join him on those training fights so they can get used to fighting together."

"A reasonable plan. I'll tell Daniel tomorrow. No one's mentioned that he'll be fighting with the champions from the other kingdoms, have they?"

Richard shook his head. "The truth is, I haven't spoken to him since we first met. Battle preparations have kept me busy and I wasn't sure if trying to talk to him would be a help or hinderance when it came to convincing him to commit to the fight."

"I'll pass the news along. It's probably simpler if I serve as his primary point of contact. Exactly which day is the gala? I've lost track and I don't want to wear him out too much the day before."

"One week from today starting at sunset. The other kings will be here earlier but there's no reason to introduce them to Daniel before then."

Lyra gave a shake of her head. "I have a bad feeling about all this. The timeline feels too compressed. I had six months to train the last hero before he ever went into the field. Daniel's only going to have one. Why is the demon king in such a rush this time?"

Richard shrugged. "Who can know the mind of a demon? All we can do is deal with what's in front of us."

He thought he sounded reasonably confident. Pity he didn't feel nearly as confident on the inside.

"You're right about that. Good evening."

She left him alone again and Richard sat on the edge of the map table. It was a relief to hear that the hero was committed, but Lyra's warning only reinforced his concern about the demon king's true plan. But, as he'd said, they could only deal with what was in front of them.

He just wished he could stop worrying about what might be behind them.

# CHAPTER 12

Danny walked through the halls toward the training ground and tried not to think too hard. He wasn't sure why the thought of putting on the hero's armor made him so nervous. It was only metal and leather; it didn't change who he was on the inside. Maybe because putting it on made it feel like he was officially the hero.

He stepped outside, paused, and took a deep breath. It was a beautiful morning. They hadn't had much rain since he arrived in this world, which was lucky since they trained outside for the most part.

"You okay, sir?" Albert asked.

"Yeah, no problem. Just feeling the weight of the moment I guess. Let's get on with it."

He strode down the gravel path and found Lyra waiting. She stood alone in their usual training spot, but there was no armor. Did she change her mind?

"No armor?" Danny asked.

"I have it in storage. You're a couple inches taller than the sixth hero's host, but I don't think any major adjustments will be necessary."

She raised her right hand and the ring on her middle finger started to glow. A moment later a white disk appeared, hanging in midair. She walked through it and vanished. A moment later she emerged with a suit of armor on a rack carried in both hands. She set it in front of him then went back in to fetch a katana sheathed in a black scabbard.

As soon as her foot hit the dirt the disk vanished. Danny couldn't stop staring at the spot where she disappeared. "What the hell was that?"

"A small pocket dimension. My ring is the key. It's totally secure and can only be opened by me. There's no safer place for the sword and armor. You'll make a ring as well, once your control is sufficient."

"Will we have time?"

"The process takes a lot of power, but isn't especially complicated. A couple of hours at most, barring any issue. You need to change."

"Right, sorry. I've seen a lot of magic, but that portal you opened was something else. I'm surprised you're allowed to keep the sword and armor in there. If something happened to you, no one would be able to retrieve them."

"Exactly. There are plenty of people like Alban Morel who would be happy to see me dead. Hanging on to the armor and sword ensures they don't do anything stupid."

Danny pulled the breastplate over his head and started adjusting the straps. It was funny. The hero's sword was a katana, but the armor was in what Danny would call a European style, though that didn't exactly apply here.

No matter how he twisted, the straps were tricky to reach.

"Let me help. This would normally be handled by a squire."

"Thanks." Lyra pulled the straps until they were snug. "Will I get a squire? Can't say I'm excited by the prospect of looking after an inexperienced fighter considering where I'm going."

"No, a squire would be dead in moments on the battlefield. I'll be filling that role for the foreseeable future. It's not like you'll have to put this on all the time, only when we're expecting combat."

With Lyra's help, the rest of the armor went on no problem. Danny made a few moves and found it wasn't too restrictive.

"Not bad. What now?"

She handed him the sword. "Go through the full range of training maneuvers. Try and get a feel for the armor. After that, I'll teach you some of the useful things mithril can do."

That sounded a little ominous to Danny, but he was probably overthinking it. He spent the next hour going through the full range of cuts, thrusts, and blocks. For the most part he had no issues with movement. The armor was either lighter than he expected or the weight better distributed. He also did some rolls and groundwork to see how difficult getting up would be. Given the protection it offered, the minor restrictions on his movement were well worth the trade.

When he was satisfied Danny said, "I'm ready to move on."

"Okay. Try drawing ether through your body like usual, only this time imagine the energy passing through the mithril before it enters your body. I think the results will impress you."

Danny did as she said and the rush of power made his knees wobble. It felt like his cells were vibrating. He didn't dare move for fear of what might happen.

"Wow. You're right, that's impressive, though I'm afraid of what might happen if I took a step."

"It's an emergency boost. I doubt even you would be able to maintain it for more than a couple of minutes. If you need to increase the power of a spell, you can channel the ether through your gauntlets or the sword. The proportional increase in power will be similar. Don't use either technique lightly. The potential damage you could do is substantial."

"That's an understatement. Should we do some sparring while I'm wearing the armor?"

Lyra nodded. "You read my mind."

And so they did. Danny made a point of letting a couple blows land on purpose to see if they hurt. Using a wooden sword, he could barely feel them. They kept going until almost dark. Danny was soaked in sweat and more than happy to let Lyra help him take the armor back off.

"Magic practice tomorrow?" he asked.

"That's right. I want you combat ready by the time the gala begins."

Danny chuckled. "I figured all I'd have to do was make small talk. Scary enough, but far from life and death."

"You're going to meet your companions and the next day we'll head into the field for live combat."

Danny read about the heroes having companions, but this was the first time anyone had spoken to him directly about it. "Who are they?"

"Eve will be joining us as the team healer. The other four

are the strongest warriors from their respective kingdoms. Just as we held a contest to determine the best host for your soul, they held similar contests to decide who would be your companions."

"Okay, but who are they? I assume if they've been chosen for such an important task they must be trustworthy. Can you tell me anything about these people?"

"Afraid not. I'll be meeting them for the first time as well. If it makes you feel better, the people chosen as companions for the first six heroes were all good and noble people. They all fought hard and some laid down their lives for victory."

That didn't really make Danny feel any better. There was a saying on Earth which went something like, "past results don't guarantee future performance." The earlier warriors might have been saints, but that proved nothing about the current ones.

"I guess we'll find out soon enough. See you tomorrow." Danny left Lyra and headed back into the castle with Albert following alongside him.

After dinner with the usual group of servants and guards, Danny headed for his room. Happily, he found Eve waiting for him and no sign of Claudette. He was both relieved and disappointed the beautiful princess had given up, for the moment at least.

"Hello, sorry I haven't been by for a couple nights. Things have been kind of crazy at the cathedral." She looked around as if worried someone might overhear then lowered her voice. "They want to have a parade for you on the morning of the gala. As a way to introduce you to the people and the other kings at the same time. I'm in charge of setting it up."

"If you're in charge, can you cancel it instead?"

"Unfortunately, that wasn't an option. What I can do is

make it as short as possible. I'm thinking from the cathedral to the castle should be enough. All you need to do is wave. Since most people know the hero by his armor, you'll be wearing it. Don't worry, I'll be right there with you."

That did make him feel a little bit better. And if he was wearing the armor and helmet no one would ever recognize him without them, so he could still walk around without drawing a crowd. It was annoying given that there was a war coming, but this sort of thing happened on Earth as well. Showing off your soldiers to make the people feel safe wasn't the worst idea.

"I'm sure it'll be fine. Do you want to come in and talk for a bit?" he asked.

"I'd love to."

Danny opened the door and motioned her through. They took up their usual spots. He would've liked to wash up, but that would have to keep until Eve left.

"Do you know anything about my companions from the other kingdoms? I asked Lyra, but she hadn't heard anything."

"No, sorry, I haven't met them. I think King Guilbert will arrive tomorrow. He'll certainly have his champion with him. You could ask for an early meeting."

Getting a feel for one of them wouldn't be a terrible idea, assuming he had any energy left after magic practice tomorrow night. "Can you arrange it for me? Lyra and I will be out of the city until evening, but maybe a dinner meeting would work."

"I can ask." Eve smiled. "The worst that could happen is they say no."

Danny hoped that was true. "Do you know a spell for telling if someone is lying? If I'm going into a meeting with a bunch of nobles, that would be a useful bit of magic to have."

"I know a divine version of the spell, but I'm not sure how a wizard would do it."

"Will you show me? It might trigger a memory. All Lyra and I practice are attack and defense spells. I understand why, but it's limiting."

Eve practically lit up at the chance to help him with his training. "Sure, it's really simple."

Danny closed his eyes to better focus. He couldn't see the ether, but he could sense it moving and every spell had a unique shape. When Eve began he knew it at once. The magic was subtle but as soon as she finished, he winced. A memory attack hit him along with the knowledge of how to cast the spell. As he'd hoped, it seemed his host had studied more than combat magic.

When the memory had settled in, he cast the spell himself. "Okay, I think I've got it. Lie to me."

"The sun is still up."

No reaction. Was that too obvious or did he screw something up?

"Nothing happened. Try telling me a lie I don't already know is a lie."

"I was born in Villipan City."

That did it. He knew with absolute certainty she was lying. He didn't know what the truth might be, but he knew that wasn't it. Danny could definitely see this being a useful spell to know. Though if by some miracle he made it back home and cast it during election season his head was liable to explode.

"It worked. Out of curiosity, where were you born?"

"A little village about a hundred miles south of here. My

parents were shepherds and I helped them until I turned ten. That's when Adonael called me to serve and I left for the Crystal Cathedral."

The magic didn't react so it must have been the truth. "I bet your parents were upset."

"Oh, no. Being chosen to serve an archangel is a great honor. They were proud of me. I've been back to visit a few times. It can be awkward since I'm technically of a much higher rank than them. They seem uncertain how to talk to me, even though I'm still their daughter."

Danny wasn't comfortable with the whole rank thing despite coming from the military. Yes, he had to salute the officers, but off base he could be Danny, not Lance Corporal Smith.

"That's tough." Man, talk about lame, but he couldn't think of anything better to say. "Do you know any other practical spells? I'd like to try and add a couple more before bed."

Her smile didn't have its usual sparkle. He should've known better than to ask personal questions and now he'd upset her. Great work, Danny. He'd messed up with the one person he felt certain was on his side.

# CHAPTER 13

The day of the parade arrived and Danny found himself back at the Crystal Cathedral for the first time since he woke up in this world. Now that he had all his faculties about him, he was able to fully enjoy the building's beauty. It was literally made of solid crystal. The walls glowed as the sunlight shone through them. He couldn't imagine how it was made though there was no question magic had to be involved.

He walked down the aisle between the empty pews. There was a door to one side of the altar that led to the back halls and eventually the garden. He'd been putting this off for a while, but the time had come to take a look at his predecessors' statues.

When he stepped into the lovely garden it came as a surprise to find Eve standing in front of the statues, head bowed, and hands clasped in front of her. He kept his distance and stayed quiet, not wanting to interrupt her prayer. Did she feel guilty? He couldn't imagine why she would since she hadn't been born when the previous heroes were summoned.

At last she made the halo symbol over her head and straightened.

"Do you come out here often?" Danny asked.

Eve jumped then quickly spun to face him. "Not as often as I should considering what the heroes sacrificed for us. I'm sorry I couldn't convince King Richard to let you meet with any of the champions early."

"I appreciate that you tried."

Danny had been moderately annoyed about the response to his request. King Richard argued an early meeting with some of them would be unfair to the ones that hadn't arrived yet. It sounded like kindergarten logic to Danny, but he wasn't in charge, so he'd shrugged and accepted the situation. There was probably some diplomatic explanation he wouldn't understand.

"I assume you'll be attending the gala tonight," Danny said.

"Of course, I'm one of your companions after all."

Danny grinned. "And yet I've been allowed to meet you early."

"Since I'm the one who summoned you, it was unavoidable. The other kings understand that. As a servant of Adonael I take no part in anything political, so that helps too."

"So am I walking in this parade or riding a float?"

"Walking." Eve's face crinkled up. "What's a float?"

Danny explained about parades on Earth. "I thought I was going to be riding on a wagon like the grand marshal."

"That sounds much more festive than what we have planned. This parade is just you, me, Lady Shael, and a company of soldiers. The people will cheer and you'll wave to them. Very simple and quick. The whole walk shouldn't take more than half an hour. Then you can change out of your armor and rest until evening. The gala starts at sunset."

"And runs until when?"

"Until King Richard calls for an end. I'd guess around midnight."

Four hours or so of chitchat and answering stupid questions plus a fancy meal. He should be able to handle that.

Eve cocked her head. "Someone just entered the cathedral. Probably Lady Shael here to help you with the armor."

"Let's not keep her waiting." Danny turned on his heel and marched back into the cathedral. It was nice to know the first hero got a statue as well despite surviving. Danny hoped to be the second to receive that honor.

Sure enough, when they reached the chapel Lyra was waiting. You wouldn't guess she was about to participate in a parade. She was wearing the same outfit she always did.

Out of curiosity he asked, "Will you be wearing a gown tonight?"

"I will. It's the one night in any given century I'm expected to dress up." She spoke in a tight, angry tone which suggested the less Danny mentioned it the healthier he'd stay. "Don't worry, they've got a fancy, stiff outfit for you to wear as well."

Danny winced, he deserved that. "Swell, we'll be uncomfortable together. Let's get my armor and go for a walk. I assume you brought the soldiers with you."

"You assume correctly. They're waiting outside. There's also a decent crowd gathered to cheer you on. They seem quite excited."

Danny wasn't surprised. One thing he'd noticed about

this world was a distinct lack of entertainment options. Of course, he was usually too tired at the end of the day for much beyond enjoying a short chat with Eve or reading a book before going to sleep. He'd actually made it through three besides the history of the heroes. Maybe that was the way it was for most people. Work all day, eat supper, and go to sleep.

While he was daydreaming, Lyra opened her pocket dimension and started pulling out the armor. Right, focus on doing the job in front of him. Pointless conjecture was just that: pointless.

They'd completed the process enough times that it only took about five minutes to strap on the armor. The helmet went on last and then they were ready. Danny led the way out with Lyra a step behind on his right and Eve on his left. Outside, twenty soldiers wearing mail covered with red tabards featuring golden lions fell in alongside them.

As soon as they moved into the street the roar of the cheering crowd washed over Danny. People lined the streets and some waved from open second-floor windows. They all looked genuinely happy to see him and his companions.

"You're supposed to wave back," Eve said.

Right, this was Danny's first parade and he was the star. Best give the people what they wanted. He raised a hand and waved. The cheering got even louder. Someone threw flowers at them. The most remarkable thing about it was that the cheer never let up for the entire parade. Everyone was going to have a sore throat at this rate.

Though he kind of enjoyed the cheering, reaching the castle wall and leaving the crowds behind was a huge relief. Knowing all those people expected Danny to save them from the demon king took away much of his enjoyment. Mostly it just made the pressure so much heavier.

"Congratulations," Lyra said. "You survived. If you can do equally well at the gala tonight, fighting actual demons will be a piece of cake."

Danny frowned and pulled his helmet off. "Did you learn that expression from one of the heroes?"

"The third used it constantly. I've never had a bit of luck when it comes to baking so I can't imagine how the saying applies, but it got stuck in my head and now I use it without thinking."

"That happens. For me it's usually song lyrics getting stuck in my head. The guys used to give me hell when I'd start humming on our way to our area of operation. They said it was distracting. Maybe they just didn't like my taste in music."

While they were talking, Lyra helped him take the last piece of armor off. It was a relief to remove the bulky suit. It would no doubt be welcome when the fighting started, but it wasn't exactly fun to wear for a walk.

Danny snapped his fingers. "Speaking of music, are guitars a thing in this world? I used to play back home and I thought it might be a good way to kill time while we're waiting for the gala to start."

"I'm not familiar with that instrument," Eve said. "What's it like?"

"Um, six strings, a resonating chamber, a neck with screws to adjust the tension, made of wood."

"Oh!" Eve brightened. "A lute."

"Similar. I've never seen a lute, but I've heard of them. Maybe I could fiddle with one and make it sound like a guitar."

"You can worry about music after the war," Lyra said. "Right now, you need to go make sure your formal robe fits. The sooner the better since the tailor will need time to make adjustments."

"Yeah, I didn't forget. Where's the fitting supposed to happen?"

"Your room. I'll let him know we're back. He'll meet you there."

"I'll keep you company until the tailor shows up," Eve offered.

"Don't you need to change?" Danny asked.

"I've got it easy. All I need to do is put on my formal robe and I'm all set."

Danny was glad one of them had it easy.

# CHAPTER 14

anny's fitting had been mercifully brief. The white robe they expected him to wear was comfortable enough aside from the high, stiff collar. The only adjustment it needed was to shorten the hem by four inches so he could walk without tripping. The tailor, a decidedly nervous man in his early thirties, had taken care of it in under an hour. As soon as he was done, he fled the area like he feared someone might throw him in the dungeon. Perhaps he shared Jean's fear of nobles. Outside of the royal family, the only noble Danny had met was Alban Morel and if he was in any way representative of the group, the tailor's fear was perfectly justified.

There was a knock on the door and Eve's muffled voice said, "It's time."

Danny blew out a final sigh, gave his uncomfortable collar one last adjustment that didn't help in the least, and opened the door. Eve was dressed in the same white-and-gold robe she'd worn when he was summoned. It suited her far better than Danny's did him. In fact, his robe looked like it was made in the same style as hers.

"Are we supposed to be twins?" he asked.

"Not twins, but you're Adonael's champion, it's only natural that your formal robe should resemble mine." She grabbed his arm and tugged him toward the noble section of the castle. "Come on, we don't want to be late."

How did she know what time it was? There were no clocks in the castle, or anywhere in the world as far as he knew. Danny was getting by with sunup, sundown, and noon. Well, whatever. He let her pull him along without comment.

"Are you nervous?" Eve asked.

"Somewhat. It's not the nerves you get before battle. This is more like how I used to feel when I had to give a book report in school, but I hadn't actually read the book."

"Try not to worry. There are no right answers tonight. As long as you're honest and show respect, the kings and other nobles will be satisfied. They mostly want to see your personality and make sure you have the will to fight the war through to its conclusion."

"If they think they can figure all that out in one evening, they're more perceptive than anyone I've ever met. Still, I'll do my best to play nice. The last thing I need is a bunch of rich, powerful people having it out for me. Bad enough I'm already on the bad side of the Morel family."

They passed Danny's usual dining room, then the library not long after. Finally, they entered unfamiliar territory. He was certain Eve had shown him this part of the castle, but he couldn't for the life of him remember what was down here.

The answer came a moment later when they strode through a pair of open double doors and into the biggest room Danny had seen yet. The ceiling vaulted high overhead, half a dozen food-laden tables were scattered about and several hundred fancily dressed men and woman milled about chatting. The whole space was lit by floating, golden lights, giving the room a mystical aura.

"Breathe, Daniel," Eve said. "If you're freezing up now, you'll never make it through the night."

"Right, no problem. What am I supposed to do now?"

"Mingle." She gave him a firm push into the room.

Mingle, she says. Well, might as well give it a shot.

Someone noticed he and Eve had arrived. They started clapping, which got everyone else's attention and soon every pair of eyes in the room was focused on Danny and everyone was clapping. He scanned the room and spotted Alban Morel standing beside another grim-faced man toward the far end of the space. It was easy since they were the only ones not clapping.

A moment later, as the gathered high and mighty closed in around him, Danny lost sight of the disagreeable nobles. Soon he found himself shaking hands, accepting compliments, and generally getting treated like a movie star at a red-carpet premiere.

Every noble, man or woman, introduced themselves to Danny. Just to be polite, he assumed, since there were so many blond-haired, blue-eyed, middle-aged people he had no hope of ever remembering all their names.

He was desperately looking for an escape when a voice bellowed, "Their Majesties, the rulers of the Five Kingdoms!"

Danny was instantly forgotten when King Richard led his family through the door. Behind them came four men wearing horribly clashing, different-colored robes embroidered with all sorts of fantastic beasts. Bringing up the rear were three men and a woman, around midtwenties, with the lean builds of warriors. Their eyes never stopped moving as they scanned the room for possible threats. They had to be Danny's companions.

He took all this in quickly then joined the nobles in performing a proper bow.

"Daniel," King Richard said. "Come join us, there're some people here that are eager to meet you."

Danny quickly straightened and strode over to join the royal party. "Majesty, or Majesties, I suppose. An honor to meet you all."

King Richard smiled. "The honor is ours. Lyra tells me you've been working hard at your training and are ready to take the field. That will be welcome. The border skirmishes have been increasing in frequency. It's only a matter of time before the bulk of the army arrives. We'll need you then more than ever."

"I'll do my best to live up to your expectations."

"I'm sure you will." King Richard put a hand on his shoulder and guided him over to the other kings. "Allow me to introduce my fellow monarchs. First is King Guilbert, ruler of the kingdom of Guilton and our neighbor to the northwest. He has the misfortune of facing the heaviest combat so far."

Danny frowned. "I got the impression the fighting was happening in Villipan."

King Richard shook his head. "Our soldiers are fighting as part of the coalition army, but the actual battlefield is in Guilton about fifty miles northwest of our border. Of course that could change at any time. We're largely fighting a defensive battle since our army can't enter the forest."

"Because of the corruption?"

"That and the trees and undergrowth make it nearly impossible to maintain a proper formation."

King Guilbert reached out and shook Danny's hand. "We'll be counting on you, Hero."

He sounded almost pitifully desperate and not at all king-like. Or what Danny imagined a king should sound like anyway. "I'll do my best, Majesty."

"But not alone! Balen, come here. Balen is Guilton's champion. Our finest warrior." King Guilbert motioned frantically toward the warriors in the back of the group.

One of them, a man about six inches taller than Danny and half again as broad across the chest came closer. He had a closely trimmed blond beard and his formal green robe strained to contain his bulk when he moved. Despite his size he didn't strike Danny as the intimidating sort. His easy smile suggested a calm, pleasant demeanor.

"An honor, Hero." Balen held out his hand and Danny grasped it. Just as Danny thought, despite his size, Balen made no effort to crush his hand when they shook.

"Likewise. Are you an arcane knight as well?"

"No, pure warrior. But have no fear, my ax has been enchanted by Guilton's finest wizards. I'll have no trouble cutting down demons at your side."

An enchanted ax would come in handy, but Danny couldn't help wondering how Balen would do without body strengthening magic.

Something tickled the back of Danny's brain. He'd never experienced anything like it. It wasn't painful exactly, but it did feel wrong.

"Daniel?" King Richard was looking at him, a worried frown twisting his lips.

"There's something…"

"I feel it too," said one of the champions he hadn't been introduced to yet. "Something unpleasant is about to pay us a visit."

"Daniel!" Lyra was headed his way. He would've smiled at the black gown she was wearing, but her two swords made him rethink it. She handed him the hero's sword. "There are demons coming."

"Demons!" King Richard said. "Here? Impossible."

"I assure you it's the truth," Lyra said.

Danny pulled his fancy robe off and tossed it aside. He'd worn his regular pants and tunic underneath for comfort and now he was doubly glad he did.

"Move everyone deeper into the hall," Lyra said. "Daniel and I will guard the door and deal with anything that shows up."

"I'm with you," said the champion that sensed the demons. "I'm a wizard and need no weapon to fight."

"In that case," Lyra said. "I would ask that you protect the royals. Should any of the demons make it past us, you'll be the last line of defense."

He looked like he wanted to argue, but Lyra had a point. There was no guarantee they could handle everything that showed up.

"I'll help too," Eve said. "My divine magic can hold the demons off for a while."

"Great," Danny said. "Use it to keep the nobles safe. Though if Alban should end up eaten, I won't complain."

Eve giggled then slapped a hand over her mouth.

"They're close," Lyra said, cutting off the conversation.

Danny got his game face on. He could feel the darkness, like a heavy presence oozing closer. They were past the library now. It wouldn't be long.

"I haven't heard anything," Danny said. "Surely they would've fought with the guards."

"The guards are carrying regular steel swords. They couldn't hurt a demon if they tried. They were likely killed before they had a chance to scream."

"That's a pleasant image, thank you. At least the guests are keeping calm."

"Other than the wizard and Eve, I doubt anyone can sense the demons' corruption. Once the fighting starts, the calmness is likely to end."

There was a click and screech outside.

"Is that..?"

"Yes. They're here."

At Danny's mental command, ether poured into his body, blazing through his veins, making him fast and strong.

An instant later, the door exploded inward followed by monsters the likes of which he'd only seen in nightmares. They had claws and fangs, scales and extra arms. Every manner of horror was represented.

People screamed behind him, but Danny blocked them out. The fight was on and he knew what had to be done.

The mithril katana sliced an arm off a demon. Unfortunately, it had three more, all of which wanted to rip his head from his neck.

With blazing speed, he cut the remaining limbs off before adding its head to be sure.

Danny had no time to savor his victory.

A black dog with glowing red eyes leapt at him.

He dodged and sliced.

Somehow the beast twisted around in midair, avoiding the keen edge of his blade.

It opened its mouth and flames roared out.

Danny didn't even think.

He threw out a hand and conjured a wall. The flames splashed against it. Through his connection to the magic, he could feel the wrongness of them. He understood instinctively that such things didn't belong in the world.

His focus on the dog monster nearly cost him when a beautiful female demon tried to run him through with a black spear.

He dodged at the last moment. The move broke his concentration and his barrier vanished. At least the dog demon had run out of flames for the time being.

Danny faced off with his two opponents. The female demon swished the tip of her spear back and forth. His eyes kept darting down to her bare breasts as they swung in time with the spear. He didn't want to look, but some force compelled him.

After one glance too many the dog demon leapt.

Danny was a second too slow and took the full weight of its body to the chest. His magic protected him, but he still ended up on his back. Before the dog's jaws could close on his throat, he sent it flying with a telekinetic blast. He'd meant to slam it into the female demon, but she was too fast.

He barely regained his feet when the black spear came darting in. He batted it aside with his sword and to his shock, the spear remained in one piece. It was the first thing he'd found that the sword couldn't cut through.

"You're going to die, Hero," the demon said. "By our mistress's command."

Why it should surprise him that the demon could speak, Danny didn't know, but it did. And she had a beautiful voice.

The spear shot in and he parried.

She had the reach advantage, but Danny was faster and

stronger. He'd lost track of the dog demon, but didn't dare look for it.

The demon smiled a sexy smile. "Wouldn't you rather put your sword down and have fun with me?"

He would very much rather do that. Danny's grip loosened on the hero sword. But only for the second it took him to realize what he was doing. He came to his senses just in time to parry another thrust.

This time he spun and stepped in, cutting hard through both her wrists. The spear and the hands that were holding it fell to the ground. He wasted no time running her through the heart. The demon immediately started melting into a puddle of black sludge.

He spotted the demon dog a moment later. It was sneaking up behind Lyra as she fought a hugely muscled four-armed demon with swords in each hand.

Danny leveled his sword, channeled ether through it, and shot a holy lance out. The spell struck the demon dog dead center and burned it to ash.

Lyra seemed to have her fight under control, so he risked a glance back at the nobles. A white wall separated them from a trio of handsome, red-skinned demons. The creatures held black daggers that they were using to cut slices out of the wall.

Danny trusted his instructor to handle her opponent and charged.

The demons sensed him coming but were too slow. After the female demon, their skills were nothing. Three quick slashes ended them.

He turned back in time to watch Lyra separate the last demon's head from its body.

Danny sensed no more corruption, but he didn't plan on

sheathing his sword until someone confirmed the threat was over.

Lyra had her hands on her knees, breathing hard. He'd never seen her so worn out after a fight. She must have gotten the tougher opponent.

"You okay?" he asked.

She straightened and nodded. "I don't recommend fighting in a corset, makes it hard to breathe. How are you?"

"Unharmed, by some miracle. It was weird, I couldn't stop staring at that female demon's chest. I shouldn't have let a nice rack distract me in a life-or-death fight, yet I couldn't stop looking."

"It's not your fault. That's succubus magic and men are especially susceptible to it. I'm guessing you forgot to raise the psychic barrier I taught you."

Danny had, in fact, forgotten all about it. "You're right, I did. Not a mistake I'll make again. She said they were here by her mistress's command."

"I was reasonably sure it was Ardent Lilly's turn and that confirms it. You can sheathe your sword, there are no more demons."

Danny did as she bid and the two of them strode down to the gathered nobles. Eve had taken a seat on the floor and looked a bit woozy. Maintaining that barrier must have taken a lot out of her.

"I couldn't cut through the demon's spear. That's a first."

"Hell-forged black iron, nearly as durable as mithril. Nasty stuff. Our enemies were armed with a great deal of it, which means this attack was no sudden thing. The demon king must have planned it for some time."

"How did he know when to send them. A spy?"

Lyra touched her finger to her lips as King Richard

approached. The king looked paler than usual. It was one thing to give orders for battle and another to have demons show up at your house. The rest of the nobles had recovered their wits enough to talk all at the same time.

"Is it over?" King Richard nodded off to one side and they put some distance between themselves and the others.

"Yes, we're clear," Lyra said.

"How, in Adonael's name, did those things sneak past our patrols and make it all the way to the capital?" the king demanded. "This is absolutely unprecedented. In six cycles no demon has made it this close to the Crystal Cathedral and now it happens before we fight the first major battle."

"They were an assassination squad," Danny said. "Sent to take me by surprise and kill me when I least expected it. I don't think we can assume anywhere is safe at this point."

"Tomorrow," Lyra said, "I'll take Daniel, Eve, and the other companions into the field. Better if we leave the capital before more of them show up."

King Richard nodded. "You planned to leave anyway, right?"

"To do some raids, but I think this will be a permanent, or reasonably permanent, deployment. Until the matter is settled, it's better if Daniel is away from civilians."

Danny wholeheartedly agreed with that. The last thing he wanted was some poor servant getting killed because of him.

# CHAPTER 15

A decidedly groggy Danny found himself standing outside the castle stable as the sun rose. After the attack, King Richard had ordered an early end to the gala, which suited Danny fine. After fighting to the death, he had little interest in polite chitchat. On the plus side, he was pretty sure he'd convinced everyone that he could do the job.

He'd gone back to his room and sealed the door with a protective spell. Even with that in place, he'd only managed a fitful night's sleep. The same thing happened to him after an intense firefight, so he wasn't surprised.

Since he was the first one to arrive, he settled down on the trunk he'd carried down. Actually "trunk" was generous. The wooden box held everything he owned in this world and wasn't much bigger than a modest suitcase. In fact, a sack would've been easier, but this was what the servants provided.

He yawned and leaned back against the cool stone of the

castle wall. As soon as he arrived at the stable, Albert had taken his leave. Reassigned, he'd said, with considerable relief in his voice. After the attack, Danny didn't blame him in the least. The demons had killed over a dozen guards before they reached the great hall. Part of him was relieved none of the guards he knew had fallen and another was disgusted at himself for feeling that relief. The lives of strangers were no less valuable than those of people he knew.

"Daniel!" Eve came trotting up. She'd exchanged her fancy robes for practical gray trousers and tunic along with heavy leather boots. She had a rucksack slung over her shoulder. It looked much more practical than his little trunk.

"Morning, Eve. Are you recovered?"

"Yes, I'm fine. There was nothing wrong that a good night's sleep couldn't fix. What about you? No offense, but you look all in."

"After-battle stress kept me up. Happens all the time. I'll be fine in a day or two and it's nothing that'll keep me from fighting. Have you seen Lyra or the other companions?"

Eve shook her head. "I came right here from the cathedral, didn't want to keep anyone waiting. I guess I needn't have hurried."

"Well, I appreciate the company for what it's worth."

She offered a bright smile, just as he hoped she would. "Me too. I've been on edge all morning. I have a lot of training when it comes to healing, summoning, and theology, but last night was my first time experiencing actual combat. It was a bit overwhelming."

That was one way to describe it. "How are you at horseback riding?"

"I can manage as long as you don't need me to do anything fancy. What about you?"

"No idea. I assume I have a memory for it in my head somewhere, but I haven't accessed it yet, so we'll see what happens when I get on the back of a horse. If worst comes to worst, I can always use psychic magic to control it."

"You have to be careful. Psychic magic comes with a lot of moral issues."

"Yeah, Lyra already gave me a lecture on it. Using mind control on animals is well within bounds, so I'm not worried."

They chatted about random pointless things for fifteen minutes before Lyra and his four companions came into view. The champions had traded their fancy gala outfits for armor and weapons. From the looks of them, they were ready for business. Lyra just looked annoyed. It was rare for his instructor to arrive this late. In fact, she had never showed up late to one of his lessons before.

"Sorry for the delay," Lyra said. "I had to brief King Richard on our route north. The other kings sat in on the discussion which meant it took twice as long as it should have. Are the horses saddled?"

"When I arrived," Danny said, "the stable hands said they were ready when we were."

"Good. We've got a fair distance to cover today. The sooner we're on the road, the better." Lyra opened her pocket dimension. "You can store your stuff in here."

Danny put his trunk inside and the opening vanished. Looked like everyone else had to carry their stuff. "I need to learn how to make one of those. I can't very well have you carrying my luggage forever."

Lyra pulled a ring out of her pocket and handed it to him.

"This is a key ring. I'll teach you how to use it to make your own pocket dimension tonight. Most of the work was done when I crafted the ring. The final steps shouldn't take you more than two hours."

Danny slipped the ring on his right ring finger, found it a little loose, and moved it to the middle. It slid on like it was meant to be there. "Thanks."

They strode into the stable and found seven saddled horses waiting. Two nervous grooms kept well away from them, as if fearing someone might find fault with their work and cut them in half. Danny didn't like innocent people fearing him, but they didn't have time to reassure nervous servants today. The best thing he could do was stay as far away from them as possible.

He went to the first horse in line, a tan one with a white diamond on its forehead. "Okay, nice horse. If you don't throw me off, I'll do my best to make sure you're not eaten by demons. That's a fair deal, don't you think?"

The horse naturally didn't reply. Danny had seen enough western movies to have a rough idea how to do this. He put his left foot in the stirrup, kicked off the ground with his right, and swung his leg over as he climbed into the saddle.

The moment he settled in, a blur of memories slammed into his brain, blotting out his vision for a moment. When they cleared, he found he knew exactly how to ride the horse. There really had to be a more pleasant way of integrating his host body's memories, but if there was, he had yet to find it. Hopefully he was just about done with them.

"Are you a nervous rider?" Balen sat confidently on the horse beside Danny. He looked much more at ease wearing a mail shirt and carrying a massive battle ax in his off hand.

"I've never ridden a horse before today. Thankfully my body knows more about it than my soul."

Balen frowned. "How did you travel around on your original world?"

Danny didn't have enough time to explain the intricacies of the internal combustion engine. Thankfully he didn't have to.

"Follow me," Lyra said as she guided her horse out of the stable.

Danny's body seemed to act on its own as he guided the horse, and soon they were trotting across the courtyard and out the open gate. A few people watched them pass as they rode toward the north gate, but no one spoke. A large, armed party no doubt did little to encourage interaction.

And then they were out of the city and riding at a steady pace down the road. Danny urged his mount up beside Lyra's. "Where are we going?"

"A fortified town called Borfin. They have a decent wall and watchtowers manned nonstop. There's no way we're camping after last night. We'd be easy targets if any demons are watching us."

"No one is scrying on us at the moment." Danny flinched when an unexpected voice spoke. It was the wizard from… Danny didn't know which of the kingdoms he was from.

"I'm aware, but an invisible imp, keeping its distance so we can't sense its corruption, is always a possibility." Lyra spoke in her usual matter-of-fact tone, but the wizard winced all the same.

"I hadn't considered that," he admitted.

"Lyra's got more experience than the rest of us combined," Danny said. "So don't beat yourself up. We weren't properly introduced last night. I'm Daniel."

"Dufour. An absolute pleasure to meet you, Hero. I was raised on stories of your predecessors and have dedicated my life to this moment. I'm confident that, working together, the demon king will have no hope of victory."

Danny nodded at the remarkably earnest speech. In his experience, soldiers tended to be more cynical than that. Clearly wizards thought differently.

"How do you like our world?" Dufour asked.

"It's interesting. Certainly much different than mine. The truth is, I've been doing little but training since I arrived. We're already farther out from the capital than I've ever been."

"Training can be difficult. I seldom ventured out when I was an apprentice. It was a long fifteen years."

And Danny had thought a month of training was bad. He couldn't imagine fifteen years of it. "When did you finish?"

"Six months ago, about a month before the champion's tournament."

That explained the upbeat worldview. He hadn't seen enough of reality to grow cynical.

And so they rode on, with only an occasional stop to rest the horses. When they dismounted, Danny found his butt and legs a little sore, but nowhere near as bad as he'd expected. His body must be more used to riding than he thought.

He'd hoped to have a chance to talk with the two companions he hadn't met yet, but Dufour seemed determined to monopolize his time. The man chattered away like some kind of fantasy tour guide, giving out descriptions of local plants and animals, history, and all sorts of other things Danny didn't care about in the least.

When the wooden walls of Borfin came into view it was a

physical relief. It would've been bad form to murder one of his companions before the battle got going, but Danny was on the edge with Dufour.

They reined in ten yards from the gate and Lyra moved a little forward. There weren't any guards outside, but on the battlements above, ten bowmen kept a close watch on them.

The central bowman said, "State your name and business."

"Lyra Shael, Champion of Villipan. The hero's party requires shelter for the night."

The guard was far enough away that Danny couldn't make out much detail, but it looked like his face had turned red. It wasn't every day the savior of the kingdom showed up at your gate. Something like that had to be stressful.

"Just a moment, ma'am. The gate will be opened presently." The guard hastened out of sight while the remaining bowmen now looked fully at ease. A couple minutes later a dull thud was followed by the heavy wooden gate creaking open.

Lyra nudged her mount through and Danny quickly followed. Inside, the guard that spoke to them bowed. "Welcome to Borfin. I hope your stay will be pleasant."

"Thank you," Lyra said. "We require rooms for the night, a meal, and a change of mounts. Have your men keep a sharp lookout. The capital was attacked last night and we don't know if more demonic assassins are in the area looking to slay the hero before he can complete his mission."

The guard's red face had turned bone white. "We'll do that, ma'am. I can show you to our finest inn and spare horses from the garrison stable are yours for the taking."

"Excellent, lead on."

Borfin wasn't a huge town, at least Danny didn't think it

was. Certainly it was far smaller than the capital. The buildings looked basically the same, one and two stories mostly made of wood with tile roofs. Loud, off-key singing emerged from one of the larger buildings along with the scent of roasting meat.

Unluckily for Danny's empty stomach, their guide led them across the darkening street to a three-story building made of stone with a gold sign over the top featuring a bed and a plate flanked by a knife and fork. Come to think of it, the librarian did mention that most commoners couldn't read. The symbols did a fine job of making it clear what the place offered.

"I can take your horses to our stable," the guard said when they'd dismounted.

"Tell the grooms we plan to leave at first light," Lyra said.

"Yes, ma'am."

"I'll give you a hand," Balen offered.

"Good idea," Lyra said. "You can show us the way in the morning."

Balen and the guard led their horses away and Lyra pushed the door open and stepped through. The common room wasn't super busy. Three parties sat at the scattered tables, all of them staring at the new arrivals. Lyra ignored everyone and went directly to the desk on the right side of the room. An older woman stood behind it, her many wrinkles deepening as they got closer. Danny offered a silent prayer that she was more agreeable than she looked.

"We need food and rooms," Lyra said without preamble. Sounded like she was in a foul mood for some reason.

"And who might you be then?" the innkeeper asked.

Lyra gave the same introduction she used at the gate.

Judging from the way her wrinkles turned into canyons,

the innkeeper was less impressed and more annoyed. "I suppose you won't be paying then."

Lyra reached into her pocket and slapped a single silver coin on the table. At least Danny thought it was silver.

The innkeeper's eyes tried to pop out of their sockets. "Platinum?"

"I trust that will be enough to cover the cost for one night."

"Absolutely!" All sign of the old woman's previous ill humor had vanished. "One room for the ladies and one for the gentlemen. You can take your meals in the common room. Thank you for choosing the Gentle Rest."

They received two keys and directions upstairs. Once again Lyra took the lead. At the top of the stairs she said, "Daniel and I will eat up here. We have some magical business to take care of."

"Oh, can I help?" Dufour asked.

Lyra shot him a baleful look. "No."

Yup, Dufour was definitely the cause of her bad mood.

Danny put a hand on the wizard's shoulder. "Why don't you guys go ahead and get started? If you could let Balen know what's happening when he returns, that would be great."

Dufour perked up at once. "No problem. Best of luck with whatever you're working on."

"Thanks." The companions went back downstairs and Danny turned to Lyra. "I suppose we're going to work on the pocket dimension thing?"

She nodded as she glared at Dufour's back. "If he doesn't get his mouth under control, he won't have to worry about the demons. I'll strangle him myself."

Despite thinking basically the same thing, Danny felt

compelled to defend the wizard. "Now, now, he's just excited. I'm sure that will wear off before long."

"It better. Come on."

"What about dinner?"

"Work first, food after. You'll appreciate it more."

Since he knew arguing wouldn't amount to anything, he followed her into the first room. With any luck the magic wouldn't take too long. With his luck, though, they'd run out of food and he'd end up eating jerky for dinner.

It took most of three hours for Danny to make his personal pocket dimension, but now he was done and could open it at will. They transferred his few belongings as well as the hero's sword and armor. Lyra said that if anything happened to her, he'd need access to them. When Danny asked what they'd do if something happened to him, she'd replied with a humorless smile and said if anything happened to him before the final battle, they were all dead anyway.

And with those words of encouragement, he took his leave. Sleep seemed more desirable than food after his exertions, so he went next door. Inside, all the companions had gathered.

Eve hopped to her feet at once. "Are you okay? You look exhausted. I brought you some food."

Danny sighed and sat on the edge of the nearest bed. "Are you sure you're a priestess and not an angel?"

She smiled at that and handed him a bowl filled with thick soup. Danny dug in with enthusiasm. As he ate, Dufour said, "Have I done something to offend Lady Shael?"

Before Danny could answer, the female companion said, "Likely your incessant chatter got on her nerves."

"Correct," Danny said. "If you can tone it down by about seventy-five percent tomorrow, you'll be fine."

He shifted his attention to the woman. "We haven't been introduced. I'm Daniel."

"Aline. I'm an arcane knight. Daggers are my specialty, throwing or close fighting."

"I'm a fair hand with a knife," Danny said. "Maybe when we have the time, assuming we ever do, we can do a little sparring."

"I'm game whenever, though I fear it will have to wait until after the final battle."

"Let's hope we both survive to enjoy it." Danny polished off his soup and turned to the last member of the group, a tall lean man with a week's worth of stubble covering his cheeks. "What about you?"

"I'm Paul, also an arcane knight. The war hammer is my specialty. I know the stories about the heroes as well as anyone, but I still thought you'd be older."

"I didn't choose the age of my host body. If it makes you feel better, my soul is a few years older."

"Forgive me, Hero, I meant no offense." Paul's nervousness clashed with his grizzled appearance.

Danny shook his head. "None taken. I'm not some jerk with a brittle ego you have to tiptoe around. My life will be in all your hands and vice versa. I'm hoping we can get comfortable with each other during this journey so when it's time to fight, the necessary trust will be there. Or that it'll be there as much as it can given that we're basically strangers."

Eve started clapping. "Well said, Daniel."

Danny didn't know if it was possible to die of embarrassment, but he wished it was right then.

Fortunately, Balen rode to the rescue. "Let's call it a night. I doubt Lady Shael will let us sleep in tomorrow."

Danny stood. "I imagine you're right."

They all shook hands and the ladies left.

Danny looked from the three guys to the two beds and back. "So who gets the floor?"

# CHAPTER 16

Danny and his companions traveled from walled town to walled town, kept to the road, and generally made their way northwest. Cutting across the country would've shortened the trip by a day, but Lyra refused to risk it. That was fine with Danny. During their stops and in the evenings, he'd been doing a bit of training with his companions. Every kingdom had different standard operating procedures. The general tactics they used were similar, but still different enough that in real combat they could cause difficulties. So they'd been trying to unify everything.

Well, Danny had been. The others played along, but sometimes he caught them glaring at each other when they thought he wasn't looking. The group needed inter-kingdom rivalry like they needed holes in the head.

At the front of the group Lyra reined in. Noon was approaching and with it their usual break time for the horses. She guided her mount to the side of the road but didn't dismount. Instead, she stared off into the distance like she was in a trance.

"Everything okay?" Danny asked.

"Yeah. I thought I sensed something, but it's gone now. Did you feel it?"

"No." Of course he hadn't been looking for anything specific and if he didn't do so, he had trouble focusing on searching. That sort of magic came less naturally for him than some did. "I'll ask Eve and Dufour."

Lyra shook her head. "If they'd noticed something they would've spoken up."

"Eve might, but Dufour's scared of you." Danny dismounted and tied his horse's reins to a handy limb.

Lyra joined him. "I'm sure he's not a bad fellow, but by Adonael he's annoying."

He had no argument for that indisputable observation. However, since he had to work with Dufour, he did his best to be patient and include the man in all their discussions. It didn't make him any less annoying, but it did keep him in a decent mood, and Danny considered that a success.

Since they usually gave the horses twenty minutes, he figured he might as well take the time to practice. He sent ether into his ring and pictured the small portal. It appeared, he reached in, and grabbed the hero's sword. He put it back, closed the portal, then repeated the process. He was getting faster all the time. The idea was to be able to access the sword at a moment's notice.

"No matter how many times I see you do that, it never ceases to impress me." Dufour ambled over. "Did you know that only one in ten thousand humans has sufficient magical ability to create a pocket dimension? Most of them are only the size of a broom closet. How big is yours?"

Danny hadn't worked up the nerve to explore the entire space—the empty whiteness gave him the creeps—but he had a rough feel for it. "About a hundred paces square."

"Do you realize how utterly ridiculous that is? It's probably bigger than every other pocket dimension in the world combined."

"I'm the hero. Doing ridiculous things is expected." Eager to change the subject, Danny asked, "Did you sense anything earlier? Lyra thought she detected something, but only for a moment."

"I didn't, but we're close enough to Fell Forest that we might start to encounter the enemy soon. If a lone monster spotted us, it likely sensed your power and fled."

"Hopefully not to find its friends. Let the others know, please, and if you have any spells that might help you detect danger, use them."

"I have been. I fear my range is simply less than Lady Shael's." Dufour glanced over at Lyra. "Is she still upset with me?"

"Not as long as you stay quiet." Danny clapped him on the shoulder and got back to practicing.

After ten draws, Lyra called for them to get moving again.

He swung into the saddle and asked, "How long until we reach the fort?"

"Three or four hours," Lyra said. "I'm hoping they can give me some up-to-date information on the enemy's current position. The main army has to be getting close, but there had been no word before we left."

With nothing better to do as they rode Danny asked, "How can the demon king's army move through Fell Forest, but ours can't?"

"Demons are undisciplined and strengthened by corruption. They have no need to fight in formations, so separating to move around the trees is no impediment to them. Every cycle they come out of Fell Forest, gather, and rush forward to meet our army on the field of battle. That's when the hero's team moves against the castle. It's usually only modestly defended when we arrive." She cocked her head as if remembering. "Except the third time, when we had to cut our way through a sea of thralls to reach the front gate. That was Baphomet's king."

"What should we expect from Ardent Lilly?"

"I wish I knew. The Lady of Lust has no particular demonic specialty, though she is known for seduction and controlling magic. She has the same power as the other lords but tends to give in to her whims. Or so I've read. Her cult is nonexistent in Villipan and I've heard no reports that the other four kingdoms are any different."

Danny found the lack of useful intel alarming, but continuing to discuss what she didn't know served no purpose. He fell silent and rode on, deep in thought, musing on potential combat scenarios based on the demons he'd seen so far. Two of them had been fairly strong, but the rest were nothing special. Mobs of weak ones led by a few strong ones seemed a likely scenario.

His mind wandered, but in the end the enemy army wasn't his responsibility. That fell to the kingdom generals, men he dearly hoped had been chosen for their ability rather than their rank at court.

He took a deep breath and frowned. "Does anyone else smell smoke?"

"There!" Balen pointed at a faint gray column of smoke rising ahead and a little to their right.

"That's the fort!" Lyra said. "How can they be under attack? There hasn't been an enemy sighted for fifty miles."

"Looks like somebody missed something," Danny said. "Do we help or do we keep our distance?"

"We help!" Eve said. "These are our allies. We can't hang back and let them be killed."

While Danny didn't disagree with the sentiment, charging in without knowing the situation was a recipe for disaster.

"We'll ride closer and take a look," Lyra said. "Acting rashly with our limited numbers and important mission would be foolish in the extreme."

That sounded like a reasonable compromise to Danny and no one else objected, though from the tightness around her eyes, Eve wanted to.

Twenty minutes later they could hear the dull thuds and shouts of battle. Lyra led them off the trade road and down a dirt path running straight toward the smoke. Danny's horse shied and that was all the warning he got.

Six demons appeared out of nowhere and leapt at them. An instinctive blast of lightning sent the one headed for his chest flying the opposite way.

Taking advantage of the momentary break, he grabbed the hero's sword out of storage. The others were hacking away at the monsters. Dufour hammered them with invisible telekinetic blasts which kept the demons off balance. Eve chanted and a white glow formed around everyone. Warmth filled Danny as the spell took hold.

A demon broke through Balen's guard and knocked him off his horse.

Aline buried one of her daggers in the creature's side, but it barely flinched as it leapt to finish off Balen.

Or it tried to anyway. Danny jumped off his horse and swung. The mithril blade cut the demon in half and it immediately started to dissolve.

He pulled Balen to his feet. "You okay?"

"Barely, thanks." Balen recovered his sword and they stood back to back.

Unable to attack the demons directly through the melee, Danny fired lances of holy energy. The divine blasts burned away corruption, but left humans and animals unharmed, making them perfect for this sort of close fighting.

Eventually magic won the day and Lyra chopped the head off the final demon. As it slowly dissolved, Danny finally got a close look at the thing. It was about six feet long, with red skin, long arms ending in claws, and a mouth like a lamprey. Ugly didn't begin to describe it.

"Mount up, you two," Lyra said. "We're moving on to the fort."

"Is anyone hurt?" Eve asked, her gaze directed at Danny and Balen.

Danny swung up into the saddle. "I'm fine. If we're going, let's go."

No one complained of any injuries and they were once again on the move. The horses clearly weren't into the plan, but they were well trained enough to go where their riders directed them.

Minutes later they reached a fort with a high wooden wall and an inner keep. It was surrounded by monsters. At least that's what Danny would call the fifty, seven-foot-tall, red-skinned brutes that surrounded the wall. Each creature carried a club the size of a small tree trunk. Arrows jutted out of their skin, but caused them no noticeable trouble.

"Fifty crimson ogres," Lyra said. "None of the scouts reported seeing any. How the hell did they make it here without someone spotting them?"

No one had an answer for her.

As they watched, one of the ogres slammed its club into the wall, rattling it but doing no visible damage. As if that was a signal, the others started pounding away. Sturdy or not, there was no way the wall could stand up to such a beating for long.

"Fifty seems like a lot," Danny said. "But I don't know how strong they are. What's our move?"

"They aren't even demons," Dufour said. "I say we attack. If we can't take a bunch of ogres, what chance do we have at the castle?"

"We can't abandon the soldiers," Eve said.

Lyra looked thoroughly disgusted by the whole situation, but she nodded. "I was planning to use this as a base for our training raids. It's not going to be of much use if it gets torn down. Daniel, stick with Eve. Everyone else, pair up."

"What about you?" Danny asked.

"I'll be fine on my own. Let's go!" Lyra kicked her horse into motion and thundered toward the fort.

Everyone else was a second behind her. Daniel eased over beside Eve as they rode. Protecting the healer was important, but he felt like it was a waste of his power. He recognized the stupidity of the thought as soon as it formed. Given her experience, it was only natural for Lyra to take the lead and if she thought he could be of more use here, then this was where he'd stay.

Danny let the others pull ahead. Balen and Dufour broke left while Paul and Aline went right. The ogres noticed them about ten yards out. The massive brutes turned and readied themselves. They didn't seem fast, thank heaven. That was a bonus.

"Sorry to hold you back," Eve said.

"You're not. Just because I'm not swinging a sword doesn't mean I can't fight." To prove it, Danny pointed at the nearest ogre and a lance of black energy shot out. The monster's head vaporized and its body collapsed. "See, no problem."

"What was that spell?"

"Disintegration beam. Takes a lot of power, but it's more precise than a fireball. One advantage of tall opponents is you can target their heads without endangering your allies."

Eve stayed quiet, but she looked pale. She'd said she hadn't seen much action before the gala. He couldn't blame her for feeling uncomfortable.

Danny blasted another ogre. As far as he could tell, they didn't have any magic resistance. Everything he'd read indicated that most demons were a little resistant to spells not of the holy magic variety. Looked like that resistance didn't extend to regular monsters.

Well, whatever. It made things easier for him. He kept a vague eye on Paul and Aline, but the others had moved to the far side of the fort, out of his line of sight. Danny had never done overwatch, but he couldn't help wondering if this was how the snipers felt when they watched the Marines going door to door.

Paul smashed an ogre's knee then crushed its skull. Aline was a blur, her daggers flying everywhere and always finding a target. Pity most of them seemed to do little more than annoy the giant monsters.

A tremor ran through the ground, making his mount shy.

"What the hell was that?" Danny asked.

Eve gripped his arm and pointed. "Look."

His eyes nearly bugged out of his head. The cause of the vibration was an actual giant. The creature looked a bit like the ogres only about twenty feet tall. It wore black metal armor and carried a massive maul that had to weigh a ton.

Danny pointed and loosed a disintegration beam.

The black beam bent away from the giant's head and struck the monster's armor where it fizzled without effect. Well, shit. That was a problem.

He looked from Eve to the giant then back. He couldn't let that thing reach the fort. One swing of its hammer would reduce the place to rubble and kill all the soldiers.

"Go," Eve said. "I'll be fine. I can raise a barrier if I have to."

She was right but he still hated leaving her alone. "Okay, but be careful."

"Says the man going to fight a giant."

Right. Once again, she had a point. Danny dismounted and activated his body strengthening. He was a decent rider at this point, but he still preferred to fight on foot.

When his body fairly crackled with power, he sprinted away, sending clods of dirt flying with each stride.

The giant looked his way as he approached, doubtless wondering what this pipsqueak thought he was going to do. Danny might not be a giant, but he could still do something.

The massive hammer swung in, seeming to move in slow motion. Danny dodged right, but still almost lost his footing from the force of the impact.

He recovered and went for the giant's right leg.

It tried to raise its foot out of the way, but Danny leapt and swung the hero's sword for all he was worth. The blade sliced through the giant's flesh like it was pudding. When he landed the foot dangled from a flap of skin and flesh.

The giant howled in pain and anger.

Danny skidded to a stop, spun, and raced toward the other foot.

It tried to hop around and put its hammer between Danny and his target but was too slow. Another slash and the giant toppled like a felled tree.

Sprinting along its back, Danny reached the base of the monster's skull and drove his sword in up to the hilt. A quick sideways yank cut its skull in half. The giant immediately started to dissolve into black goo.

Danny leapt off its back and landed well clear of the mess. He panted for breath as he scanned for more threats. Near the fort, the red ogres were stumbling around in disarray, allowing the others to cut them down with ease. The danger, it seemed, had been dealt with. For the moment.

He released the bulk of his body strengthening and strode back to join Eve. She was staring at him as he approached.

"What?"

"You took out that giant like it was nothing. When your spell fizzled, I thought you were in trouble."

"It was big, but slow. I think a smaller, faster opponent would be more of a challenge. It looks like the others are about finished. Shall we join them?"

"Good idea," Eve said. "Someone might be hurt."

Danny sheathed his sword and swung up into the saddle. Until Lyra confirmed the danger was past, he planned to leave his weapon at his side.

Lyra and the others sat on their own mounts in front of the fort's outer gate. None of them looked injured, thank heaven.

"Everyone okay?" Eve asked.

They all indicated they were.

"Once you took out the demonic controller," Lyra said. "The ogres didn't know what to do. Well done."

"Thanks," Danny said. "Are we in the clear? Also, what's a demonic controller?"

"As far as I can tell there are no more demons in the area," she said. "As for the demonic controller, it's exactly what it sounds like, a demon with the ability to dominate and control others. Ardent Lilly's followers are well known for their mastery of mental control magic. Dimwitted brutes like the crimson ogres are ideal targets for her followers."

Dufour hesitantly raised his hand as if he feared she might bite his head off. "Does that mean we should expect dominated monsters rather than undead or thralls?"

"I'm not sure." Lyra looked thoroughly disgusted. "I've been reading reports from the scouts, but I haven't spoken to any of them myself. That will have to change. For heaven's sake, we're still in Villipan. The fighting is supposed to be in Guilton."

"I guess someone forgot to tell the demon king," Danny said.

His weak joke brought a laugh from his companions and a faint smile from Lyra.

"Hello!" someone shouted from the fort wall. "Much obliged for the help. Would you be the hero and his party? I got a messenger bird from the capital telling us to expect you."

"We are," Lyra said. "Could you open the gate? You'll also need to arrange work crews to pile up the ogres for burning. Can't risk them rising as undead."

"No, ma'am, we certainly can't. Our fort isn't the most

luxurious in the world, but you're all welcome. Unbar the gate!"

There was a clunk and creak as the massive wooden door opened. Lyra led the way in and Danny finally put the hero's sword away. Being inside the walls made him feel safe, though after what just happened, he wasn't sure why.

# CHAPTER 17

After Danny and Dufour finished incinerating the ogre corpses, everyone save the soldiers on watch headed into the fort. It was late in the afternoon and dinner would be served in an hour. Before they ate, Lyra wanted to have a chat with the fortress commander, a grim, exhausted-looking fellow named Chaney. His gaunt face and sallow skin argued that his job didn't agree with him. No doubt today wouldn't help his long-term health.

He had a small office and invited Danny and Lyra to join him there. The rest of his companions grumbled about being left out, but there wasn't room in the office for all of them in any case. Danny and Lyra sat facing Chaney across a rough-hewn table.

"Where did those ogres come from?" Lyra asked without preamble.

Chaney shook his head. "No idea. I was inside the keep when the alarm went up. By the time I reached the wall, we were surrounded."

"Wait," Danny said. "You've got line of sight for what, two

miles or so? There's no way a lookout would miss fifty ogres until they were right on top of you. Were they hidden by magic?"

Chaney shook his head. "No idea. I only know what the lookouts told me. Our fort is too small to warrant a wizard which makes magic detection impossible. We're muddling through the best we can here."

"I wasn't trying to blame you or anything," Danny said. "I just want to understand."

Chaney barked a short, bitter laugh. "That makes two of us. We'd all be dead right now if not for your timely arrival. Let me offer you a proper thank-you now. We all appreciate it more than we could ever say."

"I'm glad we arrived in time." Danny didn't feel like he'd done that much and he hated taking credit for what the others had mostly accomplished.

"Have you been sending out scout patrols?" Lyra asked.

"Yes, ma'am, three times a week. None of them reported anything out of the ordinary and none of the local farms or villages have been attacked. Our little corner of Villipan has been as peaceful as you please. Until today."

Lyra ran a hand through her hair. She looked as frustrated as Danny felt. He was far from an expert on any of this stuff, even with his host's memories, but he was soldier enough to recognize that none of what had happened made a lick of sense.

Finally, Lyra stood and Danny hastened to join her. "Thank you, Commander. If you'll excuse us, we'll head to the mess hall for dinner."

"Of course. Our food is plain, but there's plenty of it to go around."

Out of curiosity Danny asked, "Do you get all your food delivered or do your scouts also forage?"

"The bulk of our staples come from the quartermaster, but our scouts will bring back a deer or boar should the opportunity present itself. Why?"

"Only wondering. Thanks for indulging me."

They left the office and stepped out into the bare, wood-paneled hall. Ten strides later Lyra stopped and turned to face him. "What are you thinking?"

"Was I so obvious? I thought I kept a decent poker face."

"I'm not familiar with that expression. Now talk."

"I think the demons are messing with your scouts. You said they were skilled at mind control, right? What if, instead of killing the scouts, they were using magic to make them forget seeing enemy formations or worse, making them think they saw something where there was nothing and vice versa. Their forces could be anywhere and we'd never know."

"Well, that's every bit as bad as what I was thinking. My fear is that they're moving their forces by magic, thus hiding them from us altogether. I'll confirm it tomorrow morning, but I can't think of anything else that would explain the ogres appearing out of nowhere."

"I thought you said teleportation magic and portal spells took too much power even for me to use. Is the demon king that much stronger?"

"Not on his own, but if he's tapped into the power of Ardent Lilly's hell via the gate in Demon King Castle, it's well within the realm of possibility. None of the other demon kings ever tried anything like this. I fear my understanding of previous cycles isn't going to be of much value this time."

"That's the nature of war. The next one is seldom the same as the last one. Is there some way to tell if the fort's scouts have been messed with? That might give us a clue about the accuracy of our hunches."

"My very plan. You talk to them and I'll handle the magic."

"Sure, but how will I know who they are?"

"Simple, just say you'd like to talk to the scouts. Tell them you want to hear about the local topography or whatever. Everyone wants to talk to the hero, we can use that."

Danny had done far worse things over the years to get intel. "Works for me."

They set out again, following the scent of something savory cooking. The keep wasn't huge and soon they arrived at the mess hall. It looked much the same as where Danny usually had breakfast back at the castle, only rougher. There was an opening in the back wall where you could see the kitchen and collect your meal. Twenty soldiers along with his companions turned to look when he and Lyra entered.

Since he had their attention already Danny said, "I'd like to talk to the scouts, maybe get the lay of the land."

Four soldiers immediately waved him over. One of them said, "We'd be happy to tell you, Hero."

Lyra hadn't been off the mark with her prediction. Danny ambled over and settled on the bench. "I appreciate it. Since we'll be operating in the area, it'll be useful to know what to look out for."

One of the scouts chuckled. "Nothing to be worried about out here, Hero. This has to be the most boring post in the kingdom. Well, before today."

"A good rule of thumb is that it's better to be over prepared than under prepared. Go ahead and tell me about it."

And so they did. Danny listened to them say nothing of

any great interest for half an hour before they ran out of stuff to say. He smiled and nodded, asking the occasional question, before finally excusing himself and joining Lyra and the rest of his companions at their table.

"So?"

"As you guessed, their memories have been altered." Lyra kept her voice pitched low. "But there's no sign of domination magic. My best guess is that they saw something the enemy didn't want revealed, they were then captured and their memories were erased. It's smart—too smart if you ask me. No wizard would ever notice if they weren't actively searching for the changes."

"And that's not the sort of thing wizards would check for as a matter of course?" Danny asked.

"No. Most forts don't have a wizard assigned to them, just like this one doesn't. The number of scouts the army employs so far outnumbers the wizards that even if they wanted to check every scout, they couldn't. This demon king is worrying me more and more all the time."

"So what are we going to do about it?" Balen asked.

"I'll send a message to the king and he can spread the word to the generals," Lyra said. "They can decide how to proceed from there. As for us, we're going to have a look around. I find I'm having doubts about how peaceful this area really is."

# CHAPTER 18

L ucky Danny was used to sleeping rough given that the beds—assuming you could call a three-foot-wide by six-foot-long wooden platform covered with a thin blanket a bed—weren't exactly comfortable. The fight had left him exhausted which also helped. After a breakfast of eggs and oatmeal, Commander Chaney had seen them off with another round of thank-yous.

As they strode away from the fort Danny said, "Do you think it was too obvious when we asked the scouts to stay at the fort today?"

Lyra shrugged, seeming not at all interested in whether they had been obvious or not. "They looked happy to have the day off, so I wouldn't worry about it."

"Why did we leave the horses behind?" Aline asked. "We could cover more ground mounted."

"Tracking's easier on foot," Lyra said. "Plus, if we run into demons, it's actually better to be on foot. Psychic attacks against the horses can cause all sorts of trouble. Fighting's hard enough without trying to do it on the back of a buck-ing, out-of-control mount."

They passed the huge black iron breastplate that had remained behind when the demonic giant melted away.

"What about this thing?" Danny asked. "Just leaving it here strikes me as a bad idea."

"Black iron needs to be dealt with carefully," Eve said. "The temple and Wizards Guild have a joint team that works to clean up black iron after the war. We can't spare the people until then."

"Pity it didn't melt away along with the demon that wore it." Tough as demons were, Danny found he liked fighting an enemy who didn't leave corpses behind.

Eve smiled. "That would be convenient. On the other hand, it would also make it easy for the demons to simply hand the armor or weapon to a new soldier and send them right back out to fight again. I don't know if leaving the gear behind slows them down any, but I like to think it does."

The conversation petered out after that and they walked on in silence. It was a remarkably pleasant day to be hunting demons. The sky was clear and the sun warm on Danny's shoulders. It felt like they were going on a picnic.

Five minutes after they passed the giant breastplate, Lyra stopped. "The tracks end here."

Danny frowned. The grass did indeed continue for as far as he could see without any sign that it had been trampled. "This basically confirms the demon king is moving his forces via portal, right?"

"I can see no other explanation," Dufour agreed. "Flying crimson ogres wouldn't be especially difficult to spot."

Danny wasn't sure if he was trying to make a joke or if he was serious. "Where to next?"

Lyra was scanning the horizon, her golden eyes glowing brighter than usual. After several long minutes she said, "That's the trick, isn't it? If they're moving by portal, the enemy could be anywhere. Last night I was thinking, why did they attack the fort now? The demons have already proven they can alter the scouts' memories as necessary to avoid detection. That being the case, why bother destroying the fort?"

"Because they don't need to be sneaky anymore," Danny said. "Whatever they've got planned for this area, they're ready to start. I bet destroying the fort was only step one."

"Right," Lyra said, her brow furrowed. "What's around here that would interest the demons?"

"It's a foothold in Villipan," Balen said. "Given how much of our combined might is in Guilton, they could march on the capital virtually unopposed. Or they could attack our army from behind while another force hits them from the front. We wouldn't stand a chance."

Those two possibilities struck Danny as both plausible and likely. Either one would be a major problem for his team. He checked the ground where the tracks ended and oriented himself so he was facing in the direction the ogres came from.

"What are you doing?" Eve asked.

"Well, assuming the ogres stepped into a portal at the origin and emerged here with a single stride, we should be able to follow the line of their tracks right back to where they came from, right?" He looked at the others, who were all staring at him. "Am I wrong?"

"Depends on the sort of portal they used," Lyra said. "At a minimum, this is as good a direction to start our search as any. Let's move."

They set out along the route Danny suggested. He felt a bit of pressure now. If he guessed wrong it would cost them time they might not have. Worrying about it accomplished nothing, so he tried to focus on the matter at hand. His skill with detection magic wasn't remotely as impressive as his destructive potential, but he was determined to help figure out what was going on.

Opening himself fully to the ether, he tried to detect any hint of corruption. Only pure energy greeted his effort. This was one of those rare times when he was disappointed not to find any lurking evil.

The group kept marching for several hours before the forest came into view. The shadows seemed especially dark and now he could definitely sense corruption.

"Is that Fell Forest?" Danny asked.

"Yes," Lyra said. "We've reached the border. Beyond those trees, men tread at their peril. If there's something here, that's where we'll find it."

"How big is the forest?" he asked.

"It surrounds the Five Kingdoms and is, I would say, a hundred or so miles deep." Lyra shook her head. "I haven't explored it since the elf-bloods arrived in this land. It has likely grown since then. There are two roads running through it, one to the east and one to the west. It's a dangerous journey at the best of times, but once the demon king arrives, only the stupidest of merchants would risk sending out a caravan."

"No adventurer would take a job guarding them either," Paul added.

"Where is Demon King Castle from here?" Danny asked.

She oriented herself then pointed north and a little west.

"That way, about three hundred miles, in the heart of the forest."

"I'm halfway tempted to forget everything else and just go there now," Danny said. "Maybe we could end this early."

"Given how differently things are going this time versus what usually happens," Lyra said, "part of me thinks you might be right. The problem is, if we march on the castle and find the bulk of the enemy army waiting for us, our combined power won't be sufficient to break through. That's why we always wait until the armies are fighting to make our move. For now, let's focus on what's happening here."

That sounded reasonable to Danny, so they set out again toward the dark forest. At the edge of the trees, a shiver ran down his spine, and when they passed under the canopy he'd have sworn the temperature dropped twenty degrees. Ambient corruption surrounded him. Trying to pick out anything specific in this was going to be impossible.

"How do we search?" Dufour asked as if reading Danny's mind.

"I'll handle it," Lyra said. "I've got a lot of practice. You all need to focus on our surroundings, so we don't get ambushed."

"I can cast an anti-corruption barrier," Eve offered.

"No, that will interrupt the ethereal flow," Lyra said. "Searching here is hard enough without another spell causing interference."

They formed a circle around Lyra and she set out. Danny stayed close to her side, the hero's sword ready, but still sheathed. If Eve's spell caused interference, then the mithril blade was sure to as well.

Half an hour later she said, "I found them. Or I found something. A concentration of especially dense corruption about half a mile northeast. At a minimum there are multiple demons present."

"Sounds like a good target," Balen said. "Do we attack?"

"Let's move closer and take a look," Danny said.

They set out again with Lyra in the lead. The elf moved silently through the forest. An impressive if pointless feat given that none of the humans were equally quiet. The closer they got to the target location, the colder Danny felt. It had to be a magical effect, but he didn't dare cast a counterspell for fear of alerting the demons.

Eventually Lyra paused and pointed straight ahead. She crept around a bunch of trees with black bark, her outline growing more indistinct with each step. Danny hastened to follow. It had gotten so dark he feared he might lose sight of her.

Danny's jaw dropped when he passed the final tree in the grove. Beyond it sat a black stone church. At least it looked like a church to Danny. There was a steeple, a stained-glass window featuring demons doing horrible, sexual things to humans, and a set of double doors he assumed led to the chapel.

"How could they have built this without anyone knowing?" Danny asked.

"I don't know and it doesn't matter," Lyra said. "We need to kill the demons and figure out the building's purpose. Eve, cast your protective spell. As soon as she's done, we charge."

"Should I put my armor on?" Danny asked.

"As soon as we take the armor out of storage, the demons will sense it and attack. Eve."

"I'm ready." Eve's hands glowed and warmth spread through Danny, dispelling the chill that had filled him earlier.

An instant later the church door slammed open and five of the lamprey demons came rushing out. The red-skinned monsters were twins to the ones that had attacked them as they approached the fort.

Danny drew the hero's sword and activated his body strengthening. Daggers whizzed past his ear as Aline attacked first. Her dagger slammed home and exploded with white light, sending its target reeling.

After that he had no time to worry about what the others were doing. Danny charged and sliced the nearest demon in half. The remaining demons roared and his companions shouted back. He cut the arm off another creature as it tried to claw his throat out.

"Daniel!" Lyra shouted. "We can handle these. Clear the chapel."

Danny didn't like leaving the others behind, but he had to learn to trust them sometime. The lamprey demons were fully engaged, leaving a clear path for him to sprint into the church.

He hadn't known what to expect, but a human-sized figure in a black dress praying in front of a black circle wasn't it.

"Step away from there," Danny said.

She spun to face Danny. The black dress turned out to be a nun's habit. An extremely sexy nun's habit with slits that ran up to her thighs and a cutout that revealed the tops of her large breasts. Who would've thought that instead of a horrible, evil creature, he'd find a beautiful young woman. Danny immediately activated the psychic protection spell. This one wouldn't mess with him as easily as the succubus at the castle.

"Welcome, Hero. My mistress said you'd show up soon. I admit I hadn't thought that I'd be the first to greet you."

"I have no interest in idle chatter, demon. Show me your true form and let's get this over with."

The nun looked at him in apparent confusion. "This is my true form and I'm no demon. I'm a priestess of Ardent Lilly and a most devoted servant. My orders were to speak with you, not to fight."

She couldn't charm him with the psychic protection spell in place. The ambient corruption did make it impossible for him to discern the truth of her words, but his instincts said she was telling him the truth.

"I'm listening."

"Here is my mistress's offer. Join us and rule the world at her side. We know you were summoned here against your will, just like all the other heroes. This isn't your world or your war. If you join our side, victory is assured as is your long and healthy life as a general in the demon army. What say you?"

Danny's lip quirked up in a humorless smile. "I have it on good authority that no demon worshipper would ally with someone bearing Adonael's blessing."

"Yes, I can well imagine who told you that. People eager to use you to fight their war. Rest assured, my offer is genuine." The nun cocked her head. "The final demon has died. Your friends will be here soon. Think my offer over. If you decide to join us, speak to any of the other priestesses. No demon will listen to you. They're too eager for blood."

With those final words she fell backwards and vanished into the black disk.

"Daniel!" Lyra sprinted over. "Are you alright? Did you defeat the demon?"

"There was no demon, only a priestess. She fled through the black disk."

He didn't have a chance to tell her any more as Lyra hurried over to the disk. The rest of his companions joined them in the chapel. Thankfully none of them appeared injured.

Balen grinned. "Looks like round two was another victory for our side."

Danny nodded. He wasn't sure if this counted as a victory since the priestess escaped. As long as no one on their side was hurt, he'd take that as a win.

"This is a portal to Ardent Lilly's hell," Lyra said. "The priestess was probably using it to power the magic she used to send the ogres yesterday. We need to seal it."

"Okay," Danny said. "How do we do that?"

"The corruption needs to be purified. You and Eve will work together to do it."

Danny looked at Eve. "What do I need to do?"

"Put the hero's sword into the portal and hold it steady while I channel divine energy into it." Eve's voice trembled a bit as she spoke.

"Don't worry," Danny said. "I've never done this before either. It'll be a learning experience for both of us."

He took a breath and slid the blade into the black disk. Or he tried to. Unlike any flesh he'd ever tried to cut, the portal resisted. Danny increased the power of his body strengthening and leaned into it with everything he had.

Desperation had started to set in when the tip finally pushed through. Heartened, he pushed harder. When six inches of the blade was in, Eve sent a beam of white energy into the mithril.

The reaction was aggressive. The church vibrated and

rumbled and the sword was nearly spat back out. Danny wrestled with it, silently praying Eve finished whatever she was doing before he ran out of strength.

A quick glance at the disk confirmed it was shrinking, though far more slowly than he would've preferred.

His body ached as he fought to keep the sword in place. His training with Lyra had been nothing compared to this. If there were more of these portals around, he wasn't looking forward to sealing them.

When the last of the darkness vanished, Danny hit his knees, totally spent. He didn't know how long that had taken, but it felt like a lifetime. "I think I'm done for this trip. What say we head back to the fort? Even some of their mediocre stew would be welcome right now."

"Good idea," Lyra said. "Outstanding work, both of you. That was no easy task and you handled it well. I'll need to send a message to King Richard. Hopefully they have at least one bird I can use."

Danny glanced at Eve. He'd been so worn out, he hadn't thought to check on her until Lyra's compliment. She was still standing, though looking paler than usual.

"How come you don't have some magical means of communication?" Danny forced himself to his feet. "Considering all it can do, that seems too useful of a spell for someone not to have come up with something."

"It's possible over short distances," Dufour said before Lyra had a chance to speak. "But the energy required is exponential, doubling every hundred yards. I, for instance, could send a message to someone I knew out to about a mile. You could probably send one five miles. Useful in certain cases, but far too limited for long-range communications."

They turned toward the door and Danny clapped Dufour

on the shoulder. "Thanks for the explanation. The things this body knows are too focused on combat. There's some history as well, but the gaps are huge."

"The hero's role is primarily combat," Lyra said. "So that's what we tested the candidates for. When the demon king is defeated, you can study history, literature, or whatever else you want to your heart's content. For now, we need to focus on the matter at hand."

She stalked out, looking grimmer than usual. It was like she thought they'd lost that fight instead of won. Danny wasn't looking forward to telling her what the nun said, that was for sure.

# CHAPTER 19

When they reached the fort, Lyra went straight for the aviary. Danny didn't bother to follow her. Their conversation could wait until he'd eaten and had a rest. They'd made it back before sunset and nothing troubled them on their way out of Fell Forest. Danny hated to make assumptions, but it seemed like this area was secure. Or as secure as possible under the current circumstances.

He and his companions reached the mess hall and found it empty. Shift change wasn't until sunset which meant they had some time to themselves. It smelled like the cook was here and busy anyway. Sure enough, when Danny went to the window to collect his stew, the grizzled, one-eared cook handed it right over along with a roll and mug of water.

Danny settled at their usual table and sighed, happy to get off his feet. He took a bite and found the stew better than expected. Must be his lucky day.

When the others had joined him Dufour asked, "What do

you think the demons are up to? Building that church and connecting it to a demon portal wasn't done in weeks or months, that likely took a year minimum to complete. Why go to all the trouble? None of the other demon kings built anything like it."

A collection of blank looks answered his question. And it was a good question. Danny didn't know enough about the past cycles to guess, but he did remember something someone, probably Lyra or Eve, told him.

"Didn't this round take longer than usual to start?" Danny said. "Do you suppose the demon king entered Fell Forest quietly, with just a few followers, and spent those missing years getting ready? It sounds like he was discovered about thirty years later than expected. You could build a few churches in that time."

"I remember the scholars at court talking about the timeline," Aline said. "If you're right, we may be in for a different fight than we thought."

On that grim note, everyone fell silent and ate. Danny glanced every once in a while at his companions. They'd fought together twice now, but he still didn't really know them. He did trust them in the vague way you trusted a new recruit who arrived to take the place of a wounded teammate, but it wasn't the sort of "no questions asked, I've got your back" trust he used to have with his squad back on Earth. Of course, that bond had been forged over months of training and combat, not days.

Danny pushed away from the table and stood. "I'm going to see what's keeping Lyra."

He returned his dishes to the cook and left the mess hall. A seeking spell led him outside and around to the aviary.

Lyra was the only one present. She stared at the darkening sky, seeming lost in thought. Before he got any closer, Danny activated a truth detection spell. Less because he didn't trust Lyra and more for practice. He'd found the more he cast spells, even simple ones, the better he got.

He hesitated to intrude. Sometimes you needed a moment to yourself.

"Don't just stand there staring," Lyra said. "If something's on your mind, let's hear it."

Danny smiled to himself. Yeah, of course she knew he was there. "Did you send your message?"

"Yes, but it was the last bird trained to fly to the capital. We'll have to wait for the next supply caravan to get more. Of course, now that I've seen the local situation, I'm less certain staying here long term is the right move."

"We were talking over dinner and the idea that the demon king arrived decades before he was discovered came up. Is it possible he spent years building churches before making his move?"

"Very possible," Lyra said. "In fact, that's one of the reasons I think we need to leave this fort. I want to check and see if there are more portals in need of sealing. My worst-case scenario is that the entire Five Kingdoms are surrounded by dozens of portals and when they're ready, the demons will attack from every direction at the same time. It would be a nightmare since the only real advantage humanity has is greater numbers."

"There's something else I need to tell you."

Lyra finally turned to look at him with her unsettling golden eyes. "That sounds bad."

"I don't know if it's bad, but the priestess didn't want to

fight, she wanted to offer me a job, as a general in the demon king's army. You said no demon worshipper would have anything to do with someone carrying Adonael's blessing. Which one of you is telling me the truth?"

"Are you putting my word against a demon worshipper's?"

Danny shrugged. It sounded bad when she put it that way. "You didn't answer my question."

"I'm telling you the truth. If you accepted her offer, you'd likely be killed the instant you lowered your guard. Ardent Lilly's followers are masters of lying. What better way to end the threat of the hero than to corrupt and kill him? Far easier than fighting him. They'll say anything, offer you anything, to get what they want, which is this world under their master's heel."

Everything she said rang true in Danny's mind. Of course, everything she said was also just her opinion, not a fact. But it did mesh with his own thoughts on the matter. He might not love this world, but he didn't want to see it ruled by insane demon worshippers either.

"Are you having second thoughts about helping us?" Lyra asked.

"I have nothing but second thoughts. Also third and fourth thoughts. But having seen the evil you're fighting, I have no intention of letting them win."

"Fair enough, if less enthusiastic than I'd like. A reluctant hero is better than no hero at all. You should rest, we're leaving at first light."

"Where to now?"

"The next fort east. We'll check the scouts for memory manipulation. If we find some, we search the nearby forest; if not, we move on."

"I'll let the others know. Make sure you eat some dinner. We can't have our leader fainting on the way."

"Elf-bloods need less food than humans, but I will have something later. Your concern is appreciated."

Danny turned and walked away. That was the only thing she'd said that he knew was a lie.

◌

Lyra watched Daniel's back until he disappeared into the keep. His doubts troubled her, almost as much as the new demon king's methods troubled her. Never, during any of the past six cycles, had anything like what he described with the priestess happened. The demon kings were creatures of power. They worshipped it, craved it, and wielded it without restraint. Subtlety was not part of their vocabulary.

She'd assumed Ardent Lilly's champion would follow the same pattern. That was clearly her biggest mistake since taking up this fight. Everything she'd assumed would happen, hadn't, and far too many things she deemed impossible had turned out to, in fact, be possible. It was an uncomfortable feeling. Her experience and knowledge had always been a source of comfort to her during these cycles. Now it seemed her greatest source of confidence was a liability and the hero's doubts weren't helping.

Her head pounded. The headache that had been sneaking up on her since Fell Forest came crashing down all at once. Lyra rubbed her temples. Daniel and everything else would keep until morning. She couldn't let his doubts affect her thinking.

She swallowed a sigh and headed for the keep. How she

missed the excitement and determination of the younger heroes. They had been so eager to please. So eager to do the right thing. Just guide them in the right direction with minimal explanation and they'd do the rest.

Those had certainly been the days.

# CHAPTER 20

Four days of hard riding across country fields and over low hills and four nights camping outside brought them to the vicinity of the next border fort. For all Lyra's talk about the dangers of sleeping outside the walls of a town or fort, the trip had been combat free. Keeping out of sight of Fell Forest had likely helped. Though even if he couldn't see it, Danny knew it was there, like a shadow at the edge of his mind.

His thoughts constantly drifted back to the priestess's offer. How could she have known exactly what he threatened Lyra with that day weeks ago? The answer, of course, was she couldn't have. It was just a coincidence. Pity knowing that helped him not in the least.

"Uh-oh," Aline said, snapping Danny out of his thoughts. "I think the demons got here ahead of us."

Considering the fort had been reduced to splinters and rubble, that seemed like a safe bet. Danny closed his eyes and activated a life-detection spell. The results were as depressing as they were unsurprising. No survivors.

"What now?" Danny asked. "We were planning on resupplying here."

Lyra rubbed her temples but didn't respond. She'd been doing that a lot lately. The stress must be getting to her. Danny felt sure he was supposed to be in charge since he was the hero, but his ignorance and lack of experience had led him to follow Lyra's lead. If it was causing her this much trouble, he'd have to step up.

"Let's take a look around," Danny said. "See if we can figure out where they came from and where they went. Once we know that, it's a matter of deciding if we hunt them down or evade them."

"We hunt them down," Balen said at once. "There are villages around here. It wouldn't take many demons to wipe them out."

That made sense to Danny. He didn't know the geography well enough to argue. The companions fanned out, but he nudged his horse over beside Lyra. "You okay? You're looking a bit rough."

"I'm fine, it's just a headache. I get them when I'm around corruption for an extended period. As soon as we're further away from Fell Forest, I'll be back to normal."

"You should wear my gauntlets or something. The mithril might help."

"You're right." She held up her hand. "Unfortunately, the armor is sized for the hero. If I tried to wear them, I'd have no dexterity at all. In an ambush, that might get me killed. Better to put up with the headache."

Danny wasn't about to argue. "Why does it bother you and not us?"

"The blood of Heaven the girls told you about, the thing

that makes my people basically immortal, doesn't mix well with corruption. While it does offer some protection, that protection comes at a price. Unless you're a dark elf, but we won't discuss them."

A piercing whistle ended the conversation. Paul waved at them from about a hundred paces east of the fort. Danny urged his horse over and Lyra came with him. She showed no sign of pain, which likely meant she was adept at hiding it.

"They went deeper into Villipan," Paul said when they reached him. "I'm no master tracker, but I'd say there are at least twenty."

Danny silently activated another spell, one designed to detect the presence of demons. The results were weaker than he expected. "Looks like more monsters with a demon controlling them. Any idea where they're headed?"

That last question wasn't directed at anyone in particular, but Paul answered first. "I fear I'm not familiar with this part of the Five Kingdoms."

"There are villages scattered all around the area," Lyra said. "Balen wasn't wrong about that. The bastards will head straight for the nearest one. Even if it has a wall, it won't hold for long."

The rest of the companions came riding up. "Looks like they appeared about fifty yards from the fort," Balen said. "One minute there are no tracks then boom, there they are. Big ones too, more ogres I'd say."

"How about a giant?" Danny asked.

"I don't think so, but it's hard to say for sure."

Danny nodded. "We'd best get after them. Hopefully we can catch up to them before they reach the town."

No one argued and soon they were thundering east at a full gallop. Probably not the wisest decision, but he really didn't want to see a village wiped out if he could help it.

After a few minutes passed and they saw no sign of the demons Lyra said, "Rein it in. If we keep this pace up for long, we'll kill the horses. On foot it'll take that much longer to reach them."

They eased back to a reluctant trot. Going so slow felt wrong, but Danny knew she was right. It wasn't like he could call in a chopper evac here, more's the pity.

"What did you tell King Richard?" Danny asked.

"I told him what we found as succinctly as I could. You don't have a lot of room to write on a message scroll. Once we deal with this batch of monsters, our next stop is the capital. If what happened here is happening everywhere, the army is going to need a full redeployment. I don't have the authority to do that. The kings all need to agree."

Command by committee was never a great idea, but in this circumstance Danny understood it. At a minimum he was glad it wasn't his responsibility.

Twilight had fallen when they spotted what was left of the village. A huge hole had been smashed in the palisade that was supposed to protect it. No enemy bodies littered the ground outside, a fact which gave mute testimony to how little the defenses had done.

Danny cast his detect life spell again and got the same result as back at the fort. The village was now a cemetery. Balen looked like he wanted to strangle someone. Everyone else just looked sick. That was certainly how Danny felt. Whatever brief temptation he might have felt to take the priestess's offer and save himself a lot of trouble had died along with all these innocent people. Bad enough that the soldiers had died at their fort, but slaughtering villagers was plain evil. But what did you expect from demon worshippers?

"We need to figure out where they went," Balen said. "We might still be able to catch them."

"It's too late and the horses need to rest," Lyra said. "We'll sleep here and in the morning head to the capital."

"And just let the monsters rampage as they please?" Paul asked. The guy had guts to talk like that to Lyra.

"If we ride through the night, the horses are likely to break a leg. Assuming we're correct about the enemy using living monsters for the bulk of their army, they'll need to rest as well. If we chase monsters instead of making a larger plan, who knows how much more damage will be done all over the Five Kingdoms. The army needs to be redeployed. We may need to sacrifice a few villages to save many more. That's an ugly truth, but it's for the greater good."

Danny hated it, but she wasn't wrong. From the grim looks on their faces, the others knew it as well. But there was another option.

"You go to the capital tomorrow," Danny said. "With your stealth and magic, you can avoid any dangers. We'll stay and hunt down as many monsters as we can. It doesn't take the whole team to speak with the king."

Now it was Lyra's turn to look grim. Looked like she didn't trust them to handle things on their own yet.

To his surprise she said, "That's not a bad idea. I can move faster on my own. Okay, I'll leave at first light while you go hunting."

Their course of action decided, the group walked through

the gap into the empty village. The damage on the inside was terrible. Homes had been smashed open, wagons crushed, and here and there a bloodstain covered the dirt. The lack of bodies was strange. Where were all the victims?

When he mentioned it Lyra said, "Crimson ogres are meat eaters."

Danny's stomach twisted. They'd been eaten? He didn't know why that seemed so much worse than the villagers just getting killed, but it did. Hopefully they were dead before the feeding began.

Retching filled the air and he found Eve doubled over beside one of the bloodstains. Danny knew how she felt. His first time witnessing the aftermath of a firefight had left him in exactly the same state. He wished he had some empty platitudes that would make it better, but the truth was nothing made it better, you just got used to the horror of it all.

When she fell silent, he went over and put a hand on her back. "Are you okay?"

"No. And I'm not sure I ever will be again. How could the archangels allow something like this to happen? I know there's evil in the world. I've read about it, heard the stories, but seeing it is so horrible."

"The archangels don't care about us," Lyra said. "Individuals, even individual worlds, aren't a big deal to Heaven. All that interests them is the greater good as it applies to the entire universe. Anything they might do, whether or not you think it's benevolent, is always driven by that cold calculus. They would sacrifice all of us in an instant if they decided our deaths would save more lives than they cost."

"How can you say such a thing?" Eve demanded. "The angels are all that is good and pure in the universe. They love everything The Creator forged."

The rest of the companions had gathered around to listen to the argument, whether because they were actually interested or out of boredom, Danny couldn't say.

Lyra looked exhausted as she rubbed her temples. "You're a priestess, so I can't fault you for feeling that way, but the truth is, the job of the angels isn't to promote good per se, but to preserve the universe. Encouraging good acts is one way they do so, but they can also be absolutely merciless when necessary. An angel would have no qualms about performing acts we would think of as evil, wiping out an entire city or nation for example, as long as they believed it served the greater good. Be grateful that summoning angels is as difficult as summoning demons. You'd no more want Adonael running around the mortal world than you would the Reaper."

Eve took a step toward Lyra, fists clenched. It looked like she wanted to knock Lyra's block off. Danny hurried to step in front of her. "We're all tired. Let's eat and get some sleep. The stress of the past couple days has put us all on edge. Things will look better in the morning."

He didn't believe that for a moment, but thought he sounded convincing.

Lyra waved a hand. "Let's find somewhere else to make camp."

No one argued and they followed her away from the bloodstains. It took a bit of searching, but the group finally found an empty, undamaged house and settled in. The place looked abandoned. Hopefully the previous owners had moved. Lucky timing if so.

There was even a simple stove and some firewood. Since no one ever complained about a hot meal in the field, Danny fired it up. He wasn't much of a cook, but figured he could throw something together. He had a huge stock of supplies stored in his pocket dimension, might as well make use of them.

Aline came to join him after he got a pot of water going. "Need a hand?"

Danny smiled. Aline was far from being beautiful with her lean, muscular build and plain face, but she had a warm, kind way about her that Danny liked.

"Sure, I never turn down help. Figured I'd make a simple beef soup. Not fancy, but filling."

He gave her vegetables to chop while he added dried meat to the now-boiling water. Once everything was simmering, he blew out a breath. It smelled good anyway.

"This isn't how I thought things would go," Aline said. "The stories made it sound like the other heroes and their companions were best friends who faced down evil without flinching, much less fighting amongst themselves. We seem to be stumbling along like drunks in the dark."

"I guess that's the difference between reality and stories. Assuming we win, I'm sure none of this will be mentioned in our own history when it's written. No sense scaring the next hero too badly. Though given the survival rate of heroes, I'm certainly nervous about the final battle."

Aline chewed her lip. "It's unfortunate that you have to fight the demon king on your own, but given the amount of corruption in Demon King Castle, we'd be useless if not dead. All I can promise is that we'll do everything we can to keep the demons outside from attacking you."

"Every little bit helps. Who knows, maybe I'll get lucky and be the second to survive."

There was no further conversation and after a silent, tense meal everyone hunkered down for the night. Danny had no idea how much worse things might become, but he dearly hoped they found some camaraderie before it happened. As things stood now, they were fighting like individuals rather than a team.

The worst part was, Danny had no idea how to fix it.

# CHAPTER 21

Danny was up and reheating the leftover soup before dawn. No one so much as flinched when he snuck into their borrowed house's little kitchen. He didn't have especially high hopes for today, but then again, how much worse could it be than yesterday? He smiled to himself. Best not to ask that sort of question lest the universe give you an answer you wouldn't like.

"I want to apologize for yesterday." Danny jumped when Lyra spoke from the doorway. "Some truths are best left unspoken."

"That's certainly true. If it makes you feel any better, I agree with your assessment. Nothing I've seen makes me think Heaven is in any way interested in us on an individual level. We're just pieces on a cosmic chessboard. Sometimes I think the way the demon lords act is more honest. They, at least, don't pretend to be the good guys."

"You're a thousand years too young to be so cynical."

"Humans grow up faster than elves, remember? Besides, no soldier survives a year in the Marines with their sense of optimism intact. You only need to be shot at by the people you're trying to help a few times before you figure things out."

"What did you figure out?"

Danny gave the soup a stir and looked up. "That the people we were trying to help didn't want our help. They wanted to be left alone to figure it out on their own. They've been killing each other in that part of my world for centuries and they had no desire to be told to stop by a bunch of outsiders."

She leaned against the wall, arms crossed. "Then why try and help them in the first place? It's not like you were summoned."

Danny smiled. Seemed she had a sense of humor and a dark one at that. She'd make a solid Marine. "It wasn't my idea. Their country had something my country wanted and the fighting was choking off delivery. We were sent in to get things flowing again. I think the last one was chromium. It might have been cobalt. I don't know. All I know is my CO told us it was a humanitarian mission. He said it with a straight face too, heaven bless him."

The soup was steaming so he shouted, "Breakfast!"

His sleeping companions jolted awake. After a few grumbles about his chosen method of waking them, they ate.

After the meal Lyra said, "I'm headed straight for the capital. Do what you can here, but if you're in danger of getting overwhelmed, don't hesitate to retreat. Everyone in the Five Kingdoms, if not the world, is doomed should you fall."

With those final words of encouragement, Lyra took her leave.

"I probably shouldn't have said anything yesterday," Eve

said. "I think she's still mad. But after what she said about the archangels, I couldn't keep quiet."

"I'm pretty sure she's mad all the time," Dufour said. "Lady Shael has been mad at me since we first met."

"It doesn't matter," Danny said. "She's got a job to do and so do we. Whoever's the best tracker will take point. We've got ogres to hunt."

His little speech didn't draw a rousing cheer, but everyone did mount up and ride out of the village. Danny refused to look back. He had enough nightmare fuel for a lifetime without burning that busted-down wall and what lay beyond it into his mind any deeper.

Paul ended up taking the lead, not that the ogres were hard to track. Their massive feet left a path of crushed grass and smashed weeds a blind man could follow. How big of a lead they had was harder to determine. Danny didn't need to say it, but he felt certain they were all hoping to catch up to the monsters before they reached another village.

"Do all the villages have walls?" Danny asked.

"All but the very smallest," Balen said. "Why?"

"Just curious. I was wondering if they got less common the further you moved away from Fell Forest."

"There are still monsters in the central regions," Aline said. "Not to mention wild beasts and bandits. Patrols and adventurers do their best to keep the numbers down, but no one's perfect."

Danny had never thought much about that sort of thing. Monsters, bandits, and demons weren't a thing on his world. At least not in the Alliance.

They kept a steady pace until the noon break. The tracks looked exactly the same to Danny, but he liked to imagine they were catching up. He dismounted and his horse immediately started nibbling at the grass on the side of the path. For his part, Danny decided to do a little magical scouting. He closed his eyes and opened himself to the ether.

As far as his senses could reach, everything felt pure. He did have a vague awareness of Fell Forest as a shadow behind them, but it didn't seem threatening at the moment. As far as he could tell, they were in no danger. Which was weird if they were getting close to the ogres and their demon master.

"Wait. Does the demon controlling them have to be with the ogres or can it give them an order then leave?"

Everyone looked at Dufour, but he shrugged. "I have no idea about the limitations of demonic mind control. My guess would be that at most the demon could give a vague order like kill everyone you meet, but nothing specific or detailed. Why?"

"There's no corruption within my range. I assume we have to be getting close, which means I should be able to detect a demon. Since I can't, I figure it must have abandoned the ogres."

"Not necessarily," Dufour said. "Some demons are skilled at hiding their presence."

That wasn't what Danny wanted to hear. What use was detection magic if the demons had a way of evading it? They were like stealth demons evading his magical radar.

After their rest Paul asked, "Do we keep following the tracks?"

"Unless someone has a better plan," Danny said. "I'm open to suggestions."

No one did, so they set out again.

Less than half an hour later a roar shattered the air. It had come from their right.

"Come on!" Balen slapped his reins against his mount's flank and broke into a gallop.

The others rushed after him before Danny could call them back. Rushing in blind really wasn't a great strategy, but it was too late now. Hanging back would've been an even worse idea, so he urged his horse after the others.

It didn't take long to find the source of the roar. Ten crimson ogres were battling six humans who were doing their best to protect a circle of four wagons. Looked like merchants and their guards. What were they doing traveling in the middle of a war?

He could find that out later. Relieving the hard-pressed guards was the priority now. Drawing the hero's sword, he angled left, toward a swordsman outnumbered by two ogres. The massive brutes were armed with wooden clubs that resembled giant baseball bats.

The nearest ogre lifted its club over its head. That worked out perfectly for Danny. He slashed across its wrists and sent both hands crashing to the ground. Blood sprayed from the severed stumps as the ogre collapsed.

He wheeled around and leapt out of the saddle. The swordsman took a hit from the surviving ogre's club and went flying ten feet.

Before the monster could follow up, Danny darted in and cut it nearly in half with a horizontal slash.

His companions were holding their own, so he shouted, "Eve! We've got an injured man."

She skirted the battle and hurried over to the swordsman. Danny shifted to protect the pair. He spotted an opening and disintegrated the top half of an ogre with a mithril enhanced spell.

"He's okay," Eve said. "Battered and bruised, but nothing

life threatening. I'll watch over him while you help the others."

Danny only hesitated for a moment. The best way to protect everyone was to end the fight as quickly as possible.

With his body strengthening at full power, Danny darted into the fight. The hero's sword made quick work of the ogres, carving through them like they were made of butter. In less than a minute the battle was over. No demon put in an appearance. That was both welcome and surprising. A creepy feeling crawled down his spine, like it was out there, invisible, watching them.

Best not to think about it.

Like a curious gopher, a chubby-cheeked bald head popped up from the bed of one of the wagons. "Much obliged for the rescue. Who might you folks be?"

Danny sheathed his sword and moved closer. "I'm Daniel, this cycle's hero, and the others are my companions. We were hunting these ogres when we heard them attacking your caravan. You do know we're on the verge of a war, right? Not exactly the best time to be trading."

"The thing is, my lord, sir, um... What should I call you?"

The merchant sounded so nervous Danny wanted to laugh. "Daniel is fine. I've never had much use for fancy titles."

"Daniel, if you say so." He made a face as if calling Danny by his name caused physical pain. "I'm Trevor, a merchant, as you've guessed. I do indeed know the perilous state of the Five Kingdoms, however, our harvest will rot if it's not collected and taken to one of the central storage warehouses. Should that happen, not only will my business suffer, but once winter arrives, there will be a lot of hungry people."

Danny frowned. Killing the demon king only to have the

people starve wasn't an especially good trade. "Where's your warehouse?"

"Rosenbar, it's a central trade hub for the northern district of Villipan. They have excellent walls and a strong garrison. Getting there is the problem. I thought the worst of the fighting was focused in Guilton, but it seems some has found its way here. I should've hired more adventurers."

Danny glanced around. His team was chatting with the adventurers while Eve helped the swordsman to his feet. The man collected his fallen sword and ambled over. "Thanks for the save. We'd have been in a rough spot if you all hadn't showed up when you did. Name's Robillard, but most folks call me Robi. I lead this band."

Danny introduced himself for the second time and after Robi got over his shock, they shook hands.

"We've got a week or so left before we reach Rosenbar," Trevor said. "Are we likely to run into any more like these?"

"No idea. Looks like there are roving bands of monsters and demons all over the place. I don't think it's tremendously likely, but the odds aren't zero either."

Trevor ran a hand over his bald head. "I've got six more teams out collecting the harvest all over Villipan. If they ran into the same trouble we did…"

"I don't know what to tell you," Danny said. "But if you'd like us to join your caravan, we'd be happy to do so. I want to check on Rosenbar. I can't imagine the demons not attacking such a high-value target."

"We'd be most grateful if you did so," Trevor said. "I'll make it worth your while."

Danny shook his head. "We're on the kingdom payroll. Consider this your taxes at work."

"Nice to see we're getting something for them," Robi muttered so softly Danny barely heard him.

"We're burning daylight," Danny said. "Let's mount up and get out of here. Guys, we're going to Rosenbar."

His announcement drew no particular reaction. It wasn't like they had a specific destination in mind. The team could hunt monsters while helping protect the caravan. If anything, Danny figured they'd make a larger target and so draw the monsters to them. Whether that qualified as wishful thinking or not, he wasn't sure.

# CHAPTER 22

Lyra kept both herself and her mount shrouded with an invisibility spell. Now that she was on her own, she didn't bother staying on the roads. Instead, she went directly cross country toward the capital. Part of her, a fairly large part if she was being honest, worried Daniel and his companions were in over their heads. But sometimes you had to throw the kid into the pond and see if they could swim. Daniel in particular was the hero and he'd ultimately have to face the demon king on his own. If he couldn't hunt down a few stray ogres without her holding his hand, he'd have no hope in the final battle.

She didn't know why she was in such a miserable mood lately. Lyra knew the way she spoke about the archangels—regardless if what she said was the truth—would upset Eve and yet she'd done it anyway. The sheer stupidity of it bothered her more than the girl's anger. Lyra's lack of self-control showed weakness she couldn't afford. Her people counted on her. Serving the kings of Villipan ensured that the refugees had a safe place to live and whatever supplies they required.

If she failed badly enough, it wouldn't be only her who suffered.

Mind occupied by grim thoughts, Lyra rode through the day. In the middle of the afternoon, she cut a line of tracks. Not ogres this time; the footprint were too small. She concentrated and sensed a faint residue of corruption. Some kind of low-level demons then. That was actually worse given that all the magic users were deployed to Guilton. Regular soldiers could kill ogres, albeit with difficulty, but even weak demons could shrug off blows from non-magical weapons.

Luckily they were headed away from the capital.

What in the world was the demon king up to? Her inability to figure that out was the source of a lot of her ill humor. He had to have a plan, something beyond merely causing chaos. Whatever it was, she feared they'd figure it out far too late.

Putting the demons out of her mind, or at least trying to, Lyra rode on. She could do nothing on her own and didn't dare risk her knowledge not making it to the king.

Six days of steady riding brought her within sight of Villipan City. It wasn't besieged by demons at the moment. In fact, she hadn't seen signs of demons or monsters for three days. Either they were avoiding the capital district or they were working their way slowly closer. She didn't have enough information to say for sure.

The western gate was wide open when she arrived and the soldiers on duty waved her through without a word. Lyra was well known in the city, but demons could use illusion magic, so there was no guarantee that someone who looked like her was actually her. How could they be so careless, especially after what happened at the gala? Just because none of the previous wars reached Villipan City didn't mean this one wouldn't.

Snarling away her frustration, she hurried on to the castle. When she reached the outer wall, the gate was closed and a full squad of ten soldiers was on duty. They weren't especially alert as they stood around chatting, but they were there.

One of them noticed her approaching and stared for a moment. "Lady Shael? We were told you were in the field with the hero."

He was likely told by gossips in the dining hall but it didn't matter. "The situation has changed. I need to speak with the king, now."

"Yes, ma'am. Open the gate!"

The portcullis clanked up and she urged her mount through. She dismounted right in front of the castle entrance and pushed the door open. It was a little after noon, so the king wouldn't be in court. Most likely he was meeting with the generals.

While she was standing there debating the best place to look first, Jean-Michael came around the corner. He didn't have his scepter with him, but he was wearing his crimson-and-gold robes of office.

"Lady Shael, this is a surprise. Where's the hero?"

"Still in the field. I need to speak with King Richard. The situation has changed."

Jean-Michael looked out of sorts for a moment. In all the years Lyra had known the human, he'd never been out of sorts.

"Is there a problem?" she asked.

"His Majesty and the other kings are out enjoying a bit of sport."

Now it was Lyra's turn to be out of sorts. "A bit of sport? The army is deployed, the hero and his companions have taken the field, and the kings have, what, gone hunting?"

Jean-Michael quailed and Lyra forced herself to relax. It wasn't his fault. It wasn't like he could stop the kings from doing whatever they wanted. And if she wanted to try and make a case for their decision, it did seem perfectly peaceful in the central district. Clearly, they had no idea towns were being destroyed and citizens slaughtered while they played about. At least she hoped they didn't or what little respect she had for the humans would be lost.

"Where did they go?"

Jean-Michael shook his head. "They took the falcons. Exactly where, I couldn't say. I believe General Gaul is still in the war room. Would you like to speak with him?"

Lyra knew General Gaul a little. He was a decent-enough fellow with a keen mind for strategy. The problem was, he lacked the authority to redeploy the army on his own. Still, if she explained the situation to him maybe together they could convince the kings of what needed to be done.

"He'll do. Please tell King Richard I need to speak with him when he returns."

"Of course, Lady Shael. I'm sure once he knows you've returned, he'll be eager to hear what you have to say."

Lyra didn't know how eager he'd be, but she felt confident he wouldn't try and avoid her. They didn't have time for that sort of nonsense. "I'll be in the war room."

She left a still-bowing Jean-Michael in the hall and made her way deeper into the castle. The war room wasn't far from the throne room. Its primary feature was a huge map of the Five Kingdoms drawn in minute detail. Every village was accounted for and royal surveyors updated it regularly. It saw little use between demon kings, but when the time for battle arrived, the map was invaluable.

She pushed the door open and found General Gaul studying the map. He wasn't a big man. Nothing about him made you think warrior. His red-and-gold uniform was crisp and his mustache perfectly oiled as was his hair. He carried no weapons and Lyra wasn't certain he knew how to fight. Not that he needed to. His job was to make plans and give orders, not swing a sword.

"Lady Shael," he said when he looked up. "I hadn't expected to see you again until after the final battle. Is the hero well?"

"Daniel's fine. He and his companions are hunting down ogres." She walked over and poked the map. "I left them here."

"That area should be free of enemy forces," the general said.

"It should be." She touched a tiny square that represented a fort. "They were attacked, but we arrived in time to slay the ogres and the demon leading them."

He hastened to mark the fort with a little red flag that indicated enemy action. "This is all wrong. Our scouting reports say the enemy is focused on the area around northwest Guilton."

"The scouts have been compromised. We found traces of memory manipulation in the ones at the fort. You can bet if theirs have been changed then the others have been similarly affected. I'd take any report that comes in with a grain of salt."

General Gaul stared at her. "How am I supposed to oversee a war if the information I receive is unreliable?"

"It's a war. You should assume anything you don't see with your own eyes is suspect."

"Even your information?"

Lyra smiled. "No, not mine. I'd die before I let a demon mess with my mind. Besides, elf-bloods are resistant to that sort of magic. Would you like me to update the map with everything I know?"

"Please do."

Lyra got busy with the appropriately colored pins. When she finished she said, "There appear to be roving bands of demons and monsters three days' out from the capital. I don't know how long we have before they move closer. My assumption, and you can take this one with a grain of salt, is that the same thing is happening in the other four kingdoms. Do you get reports from them?"

"A few, but they're more sporadic. They have their own generals, proud to a man, who are handling their internal security just as I am Villipan's." His face twisted into a pained grimace. "No doubt they're doing a better job than I am."

Taking pity on the general, Lyra said, "You're doing the best you can with the information you have. That's all any of us can do. I was completely shocked when I saw what the enemy was doing. Such a thing never happened in the first six cycles. The current demon king must have a different strategy."

"And we have no idea what it is."

"You have, indeed, grasped the crux of the situation. Daniel will get us fresh information about enemy movements," she said with more confidence than she felt. "Even if it's only local, that might give us a valuable clue."

"Any clue would be welcome. Explaining this to Their Majesties isn't going to be pleasant."

"Look on the bright side, General. It'll be more pleasant than fighting ogres and demons. Well, safer anyway."

"Indeed. Will you be staying in the capital for a time or will you return to the hero's side at once?"

"At a minimum I need to stay long enough to figure out what we're going to do. If the demon king has no intention of sending out his army, it will make planning our assault on his castle much more difficult."

General Gaul rubbed the bridge of his nose. "I hadn't considered that. I've read the histories, you know. The previous kings and generals had a much simpler time."

"It might have looked that way when they wrote those books, but when we were in the thick of it, nothing was simple."

"That doesn't make me feel any better, but thank you for the explanation."

Lyra hadn't been trying to make him feel better, she was just pointing out the facts. War was hell, literally in this case. If they didn't figure this mess out, the whole world would suffer. Lyra had no intention of letting that happen. Her people had been through enough.

One way or another, she would see them kept safe.

# CHAPTER 23

A week of riding brought Danny and his companions within sight of Rosenbar. Though smaller than the capital, it still qualified as a city. A high stone wall surrounded it and tiny guards were visible patrolling the battlements. A castle in the city center jutted up above all the other buildings. That had to be where the mayor lived.

Balen guided his horse over to Danny. "I thought we'd see more action. The demon king's forces must be scattered to hell and gone if all we came across were tracks."

"When you think of the size of the Five Kingdoms," Danny said, "there's a lot of empty space, scattered farms, and villages of all sizes. The odds of the enemy showing up where we happened to be are modest at best. I wish we could've eliminated more of the monsters, but seeing these supplies safely to Rosenbar is a good thing too."

"I suppose. But I can't stop thinking that while we were enjoying a peaceful ride through the country, there were villages being burned and innocent people slaughtered."

"If what we saw in the slaughtered village is happening everywhere, then it doesn't matter where we went and what we did—people are likely dying wherever we're not."

Balen shook his head. "That's quite a worldview. Honest though it might be, I can't say I like it."

"We have a saying in my world," Danny said. "Whether you like the truth or not doesn't keep it from being the truth. Until the army is deployed to help, six people don't amount to much, no matter how strong they might be."

Balen nudged his horse over to the opposite side of the wagon. Danny needed to stop saying things like that. Some truths were useful but not all of them.

About a hundred yards out from the city, Robi came to ride beside Danny. "Looks like we'll be parting ways soon. Wanted to thank you one last time for pulling our asses out of trouble."

"You're welcome. Having seen the aftermath of an ogre attack, I'm glad we were able to prevent it from happening again. It's a shame we couldn't do more. Until Lyra gets back with new orders, our options are limited."

"Yeah, you need to keep your expectations under control when you're an adventurer. We're not going to save the world, but we can keep our client safe and earn enough coin to look after our families. And at the end of the day, that's not nothing."

"It certainly isn't." Danny held out his hand and they shook. "Maybe we'll see each other again, hopefully under more pleasant circumstances."

Robi grinned. "The ale's on me."

The conversation ended when they reached the partially closed portcullis. It was just high enough to let someone duck underneath. There were no other wagons and only a handful of people on foot. The pedestrians approached the guards on duty first and after a brief conversation were waved through. Then it was the caravan's turn.

Since he had no idea what the protocol was, Danny was content to let Trevor take the lead.

A guard raised his hand. "Hold there. We'll need to search your wagons. There have been reports of monster activity in the area and we need to make sure none of the bastards sneak in."

"All you'll find are vegetables bound for the warehouse," Trevor said. "But by all means, take a look. We had the misfortune to run into a group of ogres on our way in. Can't be too careful with all this chaos."

While the guards got busy pulling tarps back and poking around, the squad leader asked, "Whereabouts and how many men did you lose?"

"We were seven days west of here having finished our collection run. Luckily we lost no one in the battle, though only the timely intervention of the hero and his companions saved us from a grim fate."

"The hero?" The guard looked from face to face.

"That would be me," Danny said. "You should know that demon and monster activity has spread far from Fell Forest. It's good you're on guard. Until we can get a handle on the situation, you'll need to stay on full alert. I don't know if they'll attack a city this size, but I'd be a fool to rule the possibility out."

"That's… unusual, isn't it, my lord?"

"According to Lady Shael it's never happened this way during any of the earlier cycles. I need to send word to the capital. Who's the city lord?"

"That would be Lord Mayor Droz, second son of the Droz family."

A little twinge ran through Danny's brain as knowledge of the Droz ducal family unlocked. It had been a while since that happened and he didn't find the experience any more pleasant this time. There was no particular information on the lord mayor. Heaven willing, he'd have better luck with the Droz's second son than he did with the Morel's.

"What sort of man is the lord mayor?" Danny asked.

The squad leader's expression didn't fill Danny with optimism. Probably wasn't fair to ask such a low-ranking soldier a question like that, especially about the nobleman he served.

"I just want to know what to expect before I knock on his front door, so to speak."

"He's very serious about his job. No patience for foolishness, you understand. He tries his best to live up to his elder brother's example."

"How old is he?"

The guard's expression grew more pained. "Seventies, I think."

Heaven help him. Danny looked like a teenager. No way would someone that old take him seriously, hero or not.

"All clear, sir," one of the other guards said.

"In you go. Raise the portcullis!"

The gate clanked up and they rode under. As soon as the last horse was clear, it dropped back down, all the way to the ground this time. It seemed his warning was heard and accepted. Good. The more seriously everyone took this the better.

"Are you sure you won't let me pay you something for your help?" Trevor asked.

Danny grinned. "No need. As I said, we're well compensated by the Crown. I hope the rest of your caravans make it in safe and sound."

"And I hope you have good luck at the castle. I've never had the privilege of meeting the lord mayor, but the city runs smoothly so he can't be all bad." With a final wave, Trevor flicked the reins and led his caravan down the street, leaving Danny and his companions to their own devices.

Since there was no point in delaying, Danny turned toward the castle and set out. As they rode down the cobblestone streets he said, "I'd like you to take the lead, Eve."

"Me? Why me?" she asked.

"You're the high priestess of Adonael. Even if no one believes I'm the hero, they can't deny who you are. Surely that would be enough to secure us a meeting."

She pulled a gold hoop out from under her robes. "I suppose you're right. I've spent all my time in the church studying and practicing for your summoning, so I don't really know much about dealing with nobles. Lady Shael usually handles this sort of thing."

"We can't rely on Lyra for everything," Danny said. "I'm sure you can do it. And we'll support you one hundred percent."

That drew murmurs of agreement. The rest of his companions had been fairly quiet lately. He assumed because they were from other countries and thus had no particular standing in this one. He couldn't argue with that, but it would've been helpful to have more local backup.

Fifteen minutes of traveling through the busy streets brought them to the castle's outer wall where yet more guards dressed in armor covered with red-and-gold tabards waited. At least there were only four and the portcullis was already up.

Eve walked right up to them looking more confident than he knew she felt. "My name is High Priestess Eve Carre and I need to speak with the lord mayor."

She thrust the gold hoop amulet at them for emphasis. Both men took a step back as if the amulet were a live snake. Not an unreasonable reaction to a complete stranger shoving something in your face.

"Welcome, Priestess," the right-hand guard said. "His Lordship is unavailable at this hour, but we can summon the vice mayor for you. He should be able to handle anything short of an approaching army."

She looked back at Danny, who nodded. All they needed was to send a message to the capital. Any idiot should be able to handle that.

"The vice mayor will be fine, thank you," Eve said. "Do we have to wait out here?"

"No one's allowed inside without permission from someone higher up. Sorry." Turning to his partner the guard said, "Summon the vice mayor. Be sure to let him know the high priestess is here."

"Yes, sir." The younger guard hurried through the gate.

"It shouldn't take long."

Eve stepped back beside Danny and whispered, "How did I do?"

"Perfect, though you might have been a bit aggressive with the amulet. They aren't undead in need of destroying."

"I was nervous."

Danny squeezed her shoulder. "Don't worry about it, just be gentler when the vice mayor arrives."

Twenty minutes later, the guard returned with a distinguished, middle-aged man dressed in red-and-gold robes. At a minimum the kingdom of Villipan had their branding colors down.

Danny gave Eve a little nudge and she hurried to the front of the group. The vice mayor smiled in a gentle, almost patronizing way. "Welcome, Priestess. How may we be of service to you and your companions?"

"We need to send a message to the capital. But first let me introduce you to Daniel, this cycle's hero."

Danny stepped up beside her and held out his hand. "Pleasure, sir."

After a moment of goggle-eyed staring, the vice mayor took his hand in a limp grasp and gave it a nervous shake. "The pleasure is all mine. Vice Mayor Levett at your service, Hero. If it's a message you need to send, we have six birds trained for the capital. They are yours to use as you see fit."

"That should be plenty, thanks. Just out of curiosity, where's the lord mayor?"

Levett's pained expression made Danny think he shouldn't have asked. "His Lordship naps at this time every day. He's not a young man, so it's best if he's well rested should an emergency arise. Rest assured I have both his and the duke's full confidence."

"Great. If you could show us to the aviary, I'd like to send the message out as quickly as possible. We also warned the guards at the gate where we entered that demon and monster activity has been increasing away from Fell Forest. I don't know if or how long it will take for them to arrive, but I figured you should be aware of the threat."

"I'll be sure that word is spread through the city. Follow me." Levett led them across the courtyard toward the rear of the castle.

There were guards patrolling the wall, but none on the ground. His new memories assured him that this was normal, but Danny stretched out with the ether just to make sure there wasn't a nasty surprise waiting for them around the corner.

Happily there wasn't, but he did sense something corrupt in the distance. It was vague and moving quickly but not directly toward them.

Before Danny had a chance to ask Dufour and Eve about it they reached a collection of stacked boxes, each of which held a cooing bird. They looked like gray pigeons. Messenger birds hadn't been a thing on Danny's world for hundreds of years, but he'd read about them in school. Beside the boxes was a table covered with sealed containers.

"Keeper!" Levett shouted. "We have need of your services!"

"Coming, Your Lordship," a voice from behind the birds said. Moments later, a disheveled young man in a tan tunic and matching trousers came ambling into view. He didn't look much older than Danny. "How can my babies be of service, sir?"

"We need to send a message to the capital."

"Yes, sir. Would you like me to write it or is it secret?" The keeper's offer surprised Danny given the level of literacy in this world. Maybe he was trained to do it as part of his job.

"I can write it," Danny said. "Assuming you have paper and pen."

"In the boxes on the table, sir," the keeper said. "I'll prep a bird."

The first box Danny opened held a dozen strips of paper as long as his hand and an inch wide. Not much room to work with. The second box held drying sand, and the third a fine-pointed quill and ink. He grabbed a scroll, dipped the pen, and got ready to write.

"Come on, girl," the keeper said.

Danny glanced over as the keeper tried to wrestle a bird out of its box. The pigeon flapped its wings and struggled as he pulled. Weird.

"Everything okay?" Danny asked.

"Yes sir, no problem. Sometimes they're reluctant to fly when there's a storm in the air."

Danny looked up at the cloudless sky. If there was a storm in the air it was a long way from here.

He raised his pen to write once more only to have Eve say in an uneasy voice, "Daniel, I don't think it's a storm the bird's afraid of."

Danny opened himself fully to the ether. The faint corruption he'd sensed earlier was closer and headed rapidly this way. And it felt strong.

"Shit! Dufour?"

"I sense it too." The wizard spun until he was facing northwest. "Adonael be merciful."

Tossing his pen aside, Danny joined him. The breath caught in his throat. Flying right toward them was a massive black dragon. It would be over the city in less than a minute.

"Suggestions?" Danny asked.

No one spoke as he pulled the hero's sword out of storage. He wished he had time to put on his armor, but at the rate the dragon was closing, there was no chance. Of course, even with the sword out, Danny had no idea what to do about a dragon.

A disintegration spell might drive it off.

He gathered ether, channeling it through the sword to make it as potent as possible. As soon as the dragon was in range, the gray beam shot out. It struck dead center in the beast's black-scaled chest and fizzled, much like when he attacked the demonic giant. Something was protecting the dragon.

And then it was over the city. Black-and-red flames shot from its mouth as it burned a line across the center of Rosenbar. Despite the distance, an astonishing wave of heat rolled over Danny.

A few beats of its wings sent the dragon soaring back out and around for another pass.

"It's a corrupted fire drake," Dufour said. "A full-grown adult. I thought they were extinct in the Five Kingdoms."

"Clearly there's still one left." Danny tracked the dragon's path across the sky. What he wouldn't give for an anti-aircraft rocket launcher right now. "Any thoughts on how we make them properly extinct?"

"Try holy magic," Eve said. "If the corruption is making it resistant to regular spells, that might work better. I'm bad at offensive spells, but I can try and protect us from its breath attack if it comes this way."

The dragon banked again as it turned for the city. A quick glance at the vice mayor confirmed he and the bird guy were hiding behind the pigeon coop as if it would protect them from dragon fire. Danny hadn't actually expected either man to be of any use in this situation, but the cowering vice mayor didn't exactly fill him with confidence regarding Rosenbar's leadership.

Putting them out of his mind, Danny focused on building up a charge of holy energy. That kind of magic was the most suited to mithril enhancement, so if he couldn't power it up enough to break through the dragon's scales then nothing would.

Judging by its angle of approach, the dragon would miss the castle again. That was a relief, but Danny hoped to turn it aside before any more of the city was damaged.

It was just about to pass over the outer wall when Danny loosed a beam of white light. He hit the dragon in the joint where its right wing connected to its body. The scales smoked and the dragon roared. It veered off, flying for all it was worth back the way it had come.

Danny kept a sharp lookout, but after five minutes it became clear the beast wasn't going to return. Not right away at least.

He blew out a breath and sheathed the hero's sword. "You guys can come out now, it's gone. I'm not sure how much damage was done to the city, but you might want to get rescue crews organized."

Levett poked his head out from behind the pigeon coop. "Are you sure it's safe?"

Danny wanted to laugh but caught himself. "I'm sure the dragon has fled and that people are likely to need help. I also know that the king needs to be informed of what just happened. Are the birds going to be willing to fly?"

The pigeon keeper stepped out from behind the coop. He was still holding the pigeon he'd been wrestling with. "She's calmed down now. I think she'll fly whenever you're ready."

"Great." Danny went back to the table and picked up his pen. He was surprised to find his hands weren't shaking.

"What are you going to tell them?" Aline asked.

"That a dragon attacked Rosenbar and that we're going to hunt it down before it can attack anywhere else."

# CHAPTER 24

Lyra leaned against the war room wall with her arms crossed, seething. The monarchs of the Five Kingdoms, along with a pitifully silent General Gaul, had been discussing their options off and on for a day. She'd offered her input as soon as they arrived and no one had requested that she speak again. Considering what she'd like to say, that was just as well.

No matter how they argued, there were only two options: redeploy the army into small units to hunt down the many groups of demons and monsters plaguing the countryside or keep things as they were and hope that the course of the demon king's invasion got back on its usual track. At this point, she felt confident that the odds of the latter happening were nonexistent.

King Richard slammed his hand on the map table. "We must redeploy the army! There's no other way. The last message we received from the front indicated that all was quiet. The demon king has outmaneuvered us. It's unfortunate, but delaying our response will only compound the mistake."

"That's easy for you to say," King Guilbert said. "But if we do as you suggest, and an army of demons comes boiling out of the forest, it's Guilton that will bear the consequences."

And so the circular argument began again. The other kings largely agreed with Richard, but they had sympathy for Guilbert. It could have been their kingdoms facing the threat of invasion after all. They were terrified of making the wrong move. None of them had ever faced a decision this important during their time on the throne. Which in some ways was a good thing. It indicated peace and prosperity. But it also left them mentally weak.

She was debating trying to step in when the thud of approaching footsteps stopped her. Whoever was coming, they were in a hurry.

Lyra opened the door before the messenger had a chance to knock. "What is it?"

"A scroll from the hero, Lady Shael." The trembling man held out a still-rolled-up piece of parchment.

She grabbed it. All the kings had fallen silent and were staring at her. Lyra glanced at the waiting messenger. "You may go."

He fled as if fearing she might run him through.

"What's it say?" King Richard asked.

"A corrupted fire drake attacked Rosenbar. It made one pass before Daniel drove it off. He and his companions are going to hunt it down before it can strike again."

"He can't!" King Guilbert said. "If the hero dies before defeating the demon king, we're doomed."

"If Daniel can't defeat the drake, he has no hope of beating the demon king," Lyra said. "His magic and combat skills are fully awake and he's every bit as powerful as the previous heroes and then some. The drake won't be a problem."

"All the drakes in the Five Kingdoms were slain before the demon wars began," King Richard said. "Where did it come from?"

"Does it matter?" Lyra asked. "The demon king has set up teleportation sites in Fell Forest. He can move his forces around the Five Kingdoms at will. I doubt you'll take it, but here is my advice. Redeploy half the army to the interior with orders to hunt down the monsters and demons raiding the territory. I'll rejoin the hero and we'll make our way to Demon King Castle. If an army's waiting, we'll fall back and send word to you. If not, we'll make our move. The demon king has to be providing the power necessary to activate the portals. Once he's dead, hunting down the strays will be easier."

The kings all looked at each other. Their uncertainty would've been funny under other circumstances.

At last King Richard said, "I say we follow Lyra's suggestion. This dithering has gotten us nowhere and our people are dying as we debate. Who's with me?"

After a moment of hesitation the other kings said as one, "Aye!"

Lyra was going to have to thank Daniel for sending his message. Why that had been enough to get them to think straight she had no idea, but she wasn't about to complain.

"I'm off. Best of luck, Your Majesties."

"And to you, Lyra," King Richard said.

She spun on her heel and marched out. Rosenbar was a long ride and who knew how far she'd have to go beyond that. The sooner she started, the better.

◊

The edge of Fell Forest loomed directly ahead. They'd followed the drake's trail of corruption right to it. Things would be trickier from here since the forest's background aura would hide the dragon's— no, the drake's, not dragon's—corruption. It looked like what Danny thought of as a dragon so it was hard for him to separate the two.

He fought a smile despite the danger. If his little brother could see him now he'd have flipped his lid. An honest-to-goodness dragon hunt had to be the most fantasy thing ever. Assuming he didn't get eaten, Danny would have to find some way to celebrate.

Half a mile from the trees, Danny reined in. "We should probably leave the horses here."

"If we leave them alone," Paul said, "we're liable to find them eaten when we come back."

"Someone's feeling optimistic," Aline said. "I figure the horses will find us eaten. I trained to hunt demons, not a bloody drake."

"If you want to stay with the horses," Danny said. "No one will think less of you."

He used a tone that suggested they would absolutely think less of her if she stayed behind. It wasn't that he wanted her help with the fire drake so much as he figured there would be other things around and Danny wanted to be able to focus on the drake.

"No, staying out here by myself sounds way worse. I'm just nervous."

Danny dismounted. "We have that in common. Does anyone have any advice on how best to take down a drake?"

Balen snorted a laugh. "Are you kidding? There hasn't been a drake in the Five Kingdoms for over a thousand years. No one has any idea how to fight one. Well, the elf-blood might, but she's not here."

Having Lyra here would certainly be welcome, but on the other hand, getting some practice fighting a strong enemy on his own might not be the worst thing, given his ultimate goal.

"We'll just have to figure it out by ourselves. Can one of you help me put my armor on? No way am I going into this without it."

"I can use an illusion to hide the horses," Dufour said.

"I'll add a light magic barrier," Eve offered.

While those two got busy with the magic, Danny and Balen pulled his armor out of the pocket dimension. He turned out to be every bit as much help as Lyra and soon Danny was covered head to toe in mithril. Might be false optimism, but he felt more confident with the armor on. Hopefully his confidence wasn't misplaced.

With the horses as secure as they could be, the group set out for the forest. Paul took point on the off chance there were any tracks to follow. The drake had to have landed somewhere, so it wasn't impossible to think they might find some sign of its passing.

At the edge of the trees they paused and Eve cast a protective spell over everyone. Since Danny was in his armor, there was no point in trying to be sneaky. Anything capable of sensing mithril would know they were coming. Danny drew the hero's sword and followed Paul into the shadows.

After Danny's eyes adjusted to the gloom, he peered around as if the dragon might jump out and shout, "Boo!"

It didn't and nothing else did either.

Opening himself to the ether, he tried to sense any particularly potent sources of corruption. He found one almost at once. It was about three-quarters of a mile deeper in. Not the drake, it had a different…flavor, for lack of a better word. He wasn't sure, but Danny thought it was another church.

"Do you guys sense that?" he asked.

"I sense nothing within my range," Dufour said.

"Me either," Eve added. "What is it, the drake?"

"No, I think it's one of those creepy churches. If the drake came this way, it might have been relocated via the portal."

"Is that good for us or bad for us?" Aline asked.

"Bad," Danny said. "If they sent it away, they can bring it back somewhere else. And if I'm not there to drive it off, a different city might be destroyed. That can't happen."

"Which way?" Paul asked.

Danny pointed a little bit to the right of their current path and he started walking.

Stride by stride the source of corruption grew closer. Danny focused on their surroundings. There had to be demons guarding it. No one would be dumb enough to leave something so important unprotected.

As if summoned by the thought, six of the lamprey demons came sprinting at them from all directions. The group formed a circle with Eve at the middle. No order was given, they just did it automatically. So far they were acting like a real team.

The nearest demon leapt at him, its disgusting mouth wide open, teeth flashing.

Danny rammed the hero's sword down its throat then ripped the blade to the side, cutting the monster nearly in half. It started to dissolve at once.

Not wanting to waste time, he stabbed Paul's opponent in the side. It loosed a pained howl before the head of Paul's warhammer silenced it.

Working together, the team made quick work of the demons and more importantly, no one was hurt. Danny checked his sword but no demon gore clung to it. The stuff dissolved almost instantly.

Sheathing the blade he asked, "Are we ready to keep going?"

When everyone had nodded, they set out again, every sense alert for more demons. With each stride Danny expected more to show up. The long shadows seemed to watch their every move. It was all in his head, though. The forest encouraged such paranoia. Everything felt too close, giving it a claustrophobic atmosphere.

He paused at the top of a little ridge. At the bottom sat a church that looked exactly like the first one they visited. All black, double doors in the front, and a steeple at the top. What was different were the demons outside. Instead of more lamprey demons, there were ten warriors in spiked black armor armed with saw-toothed greatswords.

"What the hell are those things?" Danny asked. They didn't trigger any of his memories. "I sense their corruption, but it's weird, unlike any demon I've encountered so far."

"They're not demons," Eve said. "They're blackguards devoted to Ardent Lilly."

"They're what?" Danny had never heard the term and apparently neither had his host. Even weirder was the fact that the blackguards were staring right at them but making no move to attack.

"Blackguards are warriors that pledge their souls to a demon lord," Eve said.

"Like paladins only evil," Balen added.

Great, unholy warriors. They were probably tough as hell too.

"Are they just going to stand there all day?" Paul asked.

"If they've been tasked with guarding the church," Eve said. "That's exactly what they'll do. They are totally obedient to their master's commands."

"Talking about it isn't going to accomplish anything." Danny drew the hero's sword and charged it with ether. "Let's see how tough they are."

He released a massive blast of divine energy. A pillar of white light exploded down from the sky and engulfed the blackguards along with the church. That had been a bit more than he was aiming for. Danny wanted to eliminate the guards, but he needed the portal functional so he could reach the drake.

When the light faded, the church was unharmed, but the guards were staggering like drunks.

"Now!" Balen leapt down the hill, sword at the ready.

Everyone followed an instant later.

Danny's first swing cut his opponent from right shoulder to left hip, armor and all. He ran another through and found he had a clear path to the church door. "I'm going after the drake!"

He didn't wait for the others to argue. A short sprint brought him to the door and he shoulder slammed it open. The inside looked the same as the first one with a black disk in the middle but nothing else, not even an evil nun to tempt him. She probably fled as soon as she heard the fighting outside.

Danny moved closer to the portal. Upon closer examination this one was different. There were runes surrounding the black disk. He knelt for a closer look and a memory twinge hit him. These were targeting runes used to determine where the portal opened. If Danny charged them with ether, they should connect to wherever the drake had gone. Or so his memories said. In the end, there was only one way to know for sure.

He took a deep breath and sent ether into the runes. They flared to life one after the other, burning with eerie crimson flames. When the final rune burst into flame, the disk changed color, now looking like a cave entrance.

Steeling himself, Danny stepped through.

&#9676;

"I'm going after the drake!" Daniel's shout put a lump in Eve's throat.

She spun in time to watch him smash through the church door and vanish inside. What was he thinking? The drake was too dangerous to face on his own. He should've waited.

A pained cry from Paul brought her focus back to the still-raging battle. One of the blackguards had gotten through his defenses and gouged a gash in his side.

Eve channeled divine energy and healed him. She could worry about Daniel later. Right now she had a job to do. Divine energy shot out from her, enhancing the companions' strength and offering them greater protection.

With Eve's magic enhancing them, the others quickly gained an advantage. Not a huge advantage, since they were outnumbered, but enough that first one then another blackguard went down. Eve was hardly a master tactician, but she could tell the others still weren't working together as well as they should be. Hardly surprising given how briefly they'd been a team. Still, their individual talent showed through and they took down enemy after enemy until all the blackguards lay unmoving on the ground.

Balen wiped sweat from his brow. "I hate fighting fanatics. They never know when to call it quits. Where's the hero? I caught a shout but couldn't make out what he said."

"He went after the drake," Eve said. "We need to catch up. Daniel will be in trouble on his own. I can't imagine why he didn't wait for us."

"I suspect he's testing himself," Dufour said. "In the final battle he'll have to face the demon king alone. This will be good practice for him. Depending on the terrain, we might end up in his way should we charge in to help."

Eve stared. She couldn't believe what she was hearing. "You don't think we should try to help?"

"I fear that any attempt to help may end up as a hinderance." Dufour shrugged. "At the very least it wouldn't hurt to take a look. For all we know Daniel is still in the church waiting for us."

She hadn't considered that possibility.

Eve turned and took a step toward the church.

Balen caught her shoulder. "Best let me go first. Wouldn't want our healer walking into a nasty surprise."

"Thank you." Eve didn't know where her head was. She wasn't thinking clearly, that was for sure. She knew as well as anyone how strong Daniel was. Worrying about him served no useful purpose, yet she couldn't help herself. Ever since his soul first appeared above his new body, she'd felt a sense of responsibility. She'd brought him here, even if she'd done it at Adonael's command.

Inside, the church was empty save for the black portal.

Dufour went right to it and passed his hand over one of the outer runes. After a moment he said, "The path is blocked. Some force beyond my power has sealed the portal. Whether the demon king or something else, I can't tell."

Eve wanted to scream but she kept herself outwardly calm. "Does anyone have any suggestions?"

"I think we just have to wait," Balen said.

Eve figured he was going to say that, but she didn't like it one bit.

# CHAPTER 25

anny's step carried him into a massive cavern. Ruddy light with no particular source filled the space. The floor was free of debris. In the center lay the black drake. Someone had fit a black metal collar around its neck. Danny assumed that was what allowed the demon worshippers to control the beast. Standing a few feet in front of it was a demon-worshipping nun.

He activated his physical enhancement spell and added both fire and corruption protections before marching closer. Now that he'd seen the collar, he had an idea. Maybe instead of killing the drake, he could free it and in so doing acquire a new ally. There was no way the drake wasn't pissed off about what they'd done to it. Of course, getting the collar off without getting eaten or burned to a crisp would be no easy task.

"I give you one last chance to join us, Hero. My mistress has been patient, but she has her limits. What say you?"

"Your demons and monsters are murdering innocent people," Danny said as he continued moving closer. "The circumstances of my coming here might have been beyond my control, but damned if I'm going to make innocent people suffer for the acts of their rulers."

"So be it. Kill him!"

The drake shifted.

Danny sprinted forward, his feet pounding so hard they gouged the stone. In the blink of an eye he reached the nun and swung. He barely registered the shocked look on her face before her head went flying.

A moment later Danny found himself hurtling across the cavern. His moment of distraction had given the drake an opening and it didn't hesitate to take advantage.

He landed with a crash of armor and rolled to his feet, battered but uninjured. The drake faced him, mouth open. Black-tinged flames came pouring out.

Danny raced to the left and the stream of fire pursued him.

He kept just ahead of it, his back getting warmer by the moment.

When the flames guttered to a halt, Danny pushed off the cavern wall and sprinted straight toward the drake. The huge, fang-filled mouth snapped at him.

He leapt, avoiding the teeth and landing on its back. His mithril sword came crashing down on the collar.

And bounced off.

The drake thrashed, trying to throw him off. Danny squeezed with his free hand and both legs. He wrapped a band of ether around the drake's neck, holding him in place.

A second blow sent a crack running along the collar.

The drake chose that moment to roll over.

Danny scrambled to get clear and failed. Several tons of scales and muscle rolled over him. The mithril breastplate creaked but held. His left arm was wrenched and he was pretty sure it popped out of its socket.

Most importantly, Danny maintained his grip on the hero's sword. As soon as the drake rolled off him, Danny scrambled to his feet and leapt back on the drake's neck. A final blow snapped the collar in half. He yanked hard, pulling spikes out of the drake's neck and tossing the pieces aside.

Danny leapt clear and raised the sword, ready to resume the fight should it be necessary.

For its part, the drake roared and thrashed, spewing flames at random. An effort of will conjured a barrier in front of Danny. Stray flames splashed over it.

Slowly, over the course of about five minutes, the drake calmed. Its breath came in huffs and puffs. After a few wheezing breaths it lay flat on the cavern floor and stared at Danny. He hesitated for a moment then lowered his shield.

When no burst of flame assaulted him, Danny moved a bit closer. "Are you okay now?"

He felt kind of stupid talking to the drake. Could the thing even understand him?

"My mind is free. Thank you, Hero." The drake's voice was a deep, bass rumble that vibrated Danny's bones.

"You're welcome. Sorry I couldn't be gentler taking the collar off. The spikes were really jammed in tight."

"The cursed black iron is the bane of all life. Better a moment of pain than an eternity of servitude."

Looked like more than a moment of pain to Danny, but he didn't comment. "Now that you're free, is there any chance I can talk you into helping me kill the demon king?"

"Much as I would like to, I'll be dead in a few hours. The collar corrupted my flesh and without it I can't sustain my life. When the time comes, I'll need you to remove my head so that I don't rise as a demonic thrall. I've done enough damage to the world as it is. Will you do me this final favor, Hero?"

Danny nodded at once. He had no desire to see the drake transformed into some kind of demon. Fighting a living one was hard enough, he couldn't imagine fighting a demonic version. First he needed to fix up his shoulder. While he wasn't as skilled as Eve, Danny knew enough about holy magic to handle something that simple and he got the ether flowing.

"Thank you. Having freed me from the collar, I hate to ask more of you. To show my gratitude, I have two gifts to offer." A white disk appeared in midair. It looked just like the one that led to Danny's pocket dimension. A silver ring and a sword hilt without a blade flew out and landed in front of Danny. "Accept these treasures as payment for your services."

Danny activated a spell that let him see magical auras. The ring blazed like the sun but the hilt appeared powerless. "Are you sure?"

"I am. When I die, my storage area dies with me and the treasures within would be lost forever. Better I give them to an honorable warrior that they might be used for a righteous cause. I will explain how to use them. Attend well."

Danny gave the drake his full attention. "Before we begin, do you have a name?"

"Merrok. And you?"

"Daniel. I wish we could've met under better circumstances. You seem a decent fellow."

"As do you. Most humans want nothing more than to slay my kind and claim our treasure and territory."

Danny smiled at that. "If it's any consolation, we like to

slay our own kind for treasure and territory as well. It's sort of a broad human trait. Please don't take it personally."

It took him a moment to realize the huffing rumble coming from Merrok was laughter. "Amusing as this conversation is, my time grows short and you must be taught."

"Right," Danny said. "Let's start with the ring. I've never seen anything shine so brightly in the ether."

"Nor are you ever likely to again. That is a star ring, brought from Heaven by the elves, the true elves, when they first came to this world. It's blessed by the archangels using a fragment of The Creator's power. It has the ability to warp reality, granting nearly any wish you might desire."

Danny stared at the small silver ring resting in his palm. So much power in such a little package. "Can I use this to kill the demon king?"

"No," Merrok said. "The demon king is protected by the blessing of a demon lord and can only be slain in direct combat."

"Great, so the one thing I really need it to do, it can't do."

"I did say *almost* any wish."

He did at that. Well, there was one more option. "Can it bring me back to life if the demon king kills me like the other heroes?"

"That is well within its power."

"So, I just put the ring on and say what I wish?"

"Yes. But think hard how you want to word your wish. The magic is very tricky. Whatever you say will become reality and if there's a way to twist your words it will."

Danny slipped the ring on. That was some extra pressure he didn't need. Composing himself, he thought hard about what he wanted. At last, he said, "If I'm killed I wish to be brought back to life in a safe place one day later."

It felt like electricity was running through his veins. Nothing like that had ever happened before. When it stopped, the ring disintegrated. Did it work? If it did, he'd have a second chance should the demon king defeat him. Hopefully it wouldn't come to that.

Merrok coughed, a great wheezing gasp. "We must hurry. Pick up the hilt."

Danny obliged. The decorative basket hilt felt good in his hand—smooth, with just the right amount of heft. "Is this mithril?"

"Indeed, this is another treasure of the ancient elves, their half-elven progeny this time. This is an etherblade. Draw ether through the bottom of the hilt. Make sure the top is pointed away from you."

Danny obliged and an instant later a three-foot-long beam of white light shot out. "Holy shit!"

He swung it around. The blade was weightless and made no sound. That would take some getting used to.

"The mithril concentrates and focuses ether into a disin-tegration beam. It will maintain itself until you form a cap of ether at the base of the hilt to stop the energy flow. This weapon is almost as effective as mithril and should serve you well as a backup. But be aware that should you take it into a magic dead zone where the ether doesn't flow, you will be unarmed."

Danny made a cap of ether over the bottom of the hilt and the blade vanished. "Wouldn't an enemy wizard be able to disarm me as well?"

"That is another danger, but the wizard would have to be exceptionally skilled to be able to block the flow of ether while hitting a moving target. Assuming they knew how to deactivate the blade in the first place." Merrok's face scrunched up and he lowered his head so it rested on the floor. "It's time, Hero."

Danny grimaced and put the hilt in his pocket dimension. He hated having to do this. Merrok was entirely too kind to have his head cut off. He deserved better, not that humanity was likely to forgive him for the attack on Rosenbar, even if he had been under the demon's control.

Taking up his mithril blade, Danny strode over. If he had to do this, he could make it quick and clean. Merrok deserved that much.

"I'm glad I got to meet you, Merrok."

"Likewise, Daniel."

The sword went up. "You can call me Danny."

With a single powerful blow, he severed his new friend's head from his neck. The blade continued into the stone, burying itself four inches deep.

Blowing out a breath, Danny yanked it free and used its keen edge to slice off one of Merrok's scales. That should be proof enough that the deed was done.

Sheathing his blade, he walked back to the portal. Energy flowed and soon all the runes had lit up and he could see his companions standing around the church waiting for him. A single stride carried Danny from the cavern to the church.

"Daniel!" Eve hurried over. "Are you hurt? What happened?"

Danny had no intention of sharing the details of his conversation with Merrok. Somehow it felt like sharing it would make it less special.

"I'm okay. It was a difficult fight, but I won." He showed them the scale. "A priestess was controlling the drake. I think they planned to send it around burning cities."

"Sounds about right." Dufour clapped him on the shoulder. "You gave us quite a scare when you ran off on your own."

"Sorry about that. It's just as well you didn't go. The corruption was crazy thick. Without mithril armor, you guys might have been in trouble."

"All's well that ends well, I guess," Aline said. "What now?"

"Now Eve and I seal the gate and we get out of here. When Lyra returns, she'll likely start looking for us in Rosenbar. I'm sure the lord mayor, or his assistant anyway, will want to know the drake has been dealt with as well."

Eve favored him with a searching look, but finally she nodded and they got to work. Sealing the gate went more smoothly this time. Maybe their previous experience helped. Once that final task was complete, everyone was eager to put Fell Forest behind them, for the time being at least.

# CHAPTER 26

Danny almost felt light as he and his companions rode back to Rosenbar. He was still nervous of course, but knowing he had a second chance in his back pocket took some of the pressure off. Death was less scary if it wasn't final.

He glanced at the others. Eve was still grumpy about him running off to fight the drake on his own. Understandable, but in the end the hero and the demon king would face off one on one. Danny needed to practice. If he got too comfortable trusting the others to have his back, it would leave him open during the final battle. And while he had a second or maybe third life waiting for him, he'd be just as happy to never need it.

"There it is!" Paul said.

The walls of Rosenbar rose in the distance. There was once again no sign of demons or monsters. In fact, they hadn't encountered any threats the entire way back. Sealing the church's portal might have made it hard for the demon king to send monsters to this area. That was Danny's working theory anyway. Whatever the reason, it should make things easier on the locals.

An hour later they were trotting down the main street toward the mayor's castle. They were on the opposite side from where Merrok attacked. That suited Danny fine as he'd seen all the burned-out houses and dead bodies he needed to back on Earth.

On this side of the city, life seemed basically normal. People were out and about running errands. A few waved but most shied away from them. Perfectly natural reaction to a group of armed individuals.

When they reached the castle gate, the guards on duty waved them right through. Danny paused long enough to ask, "Has Lady Shael arrived?"

"Yes, my lord. She arrived yesterday. She'd ridden her horse nearly to death."

Lyra must have been more anxious to rejoin them than Danny expected. "Thanks. The drake's dead. Feel free to spread the word."

The guards slumped a bit in obvious relief. "Wonderful news, my lord. The people have been terrified it might return at any moment to finish what it started. His Lordship will be most pleased as well."

Danny nodded a farewell and nudged his horse into motion again.

"Do you think it's okay to tell the guards before the lord mayor?" Eve asked.

"I don't see what difference it makes," Danny said. "I'm sure that by the end of the day the message will be spread throughout the city. Why not make an early start?"

"Mostly because nobles are prickly about their privileges," Dufour said. "I've known some good ones and some bad ones, but to a person, they all expect to be the first informed whenever anything important happens."

Danny shrugged. "Well, it's not like I can un-mention it. Let's just find Lyra. I want to know what the plan is."

"I like your optimism," Balen said. "You think all five kings will agree on a new plan? They barely agreed on the first one."

"Given the alternative, which is monsters and demons running around unopposed doing heaven only knows how much damage to innocent people, I dearly hope you're wrong about their stubbornness." Danny dismounted in front of the keep and tied his horse to the iron ring hammered into it for that purpose.

The others joined him and they headed for the doors. The guards on duty saluted as they approached then pulled the doors open. "Welcome back, my lord," the right-hand guard said. "Everyone will be pleased to see you've returned unharmed. Announce the hero's return."

The other guard ducked inside, presumably to let the powers that be know they'd arrived.

"Was it a hard fight?" the remaining guard asked.

"Hard enough," Danny said. "If you can avoid fighting a corrupted fire drake, I recommend doing so."

The guard's laugh sounded a bit hysterical. "Rest assured, my lord, that I have no intention of ever trying such a thing."

Danny clapped him on the shoulder and grinned. "Very wise."

A few minutes later Vice Mayor Levett and Lyra came striding toward them. Danny wasn't sure he'd ever seen her looking more tired. Her golden eyes were dim and while her pale skin remained flawless, he thought some of the color had leeched out of it.

"Welcome back, Hero," Levett said. "The drake?"

"Dead. Any chance we can have this conversation inside? We're tired and could use a freshly cooked meal."

"Of course, of course," Levett said. "The cooks will prepare whatever you'd like. It's nearly dinner time anyway. We'll eat in my private quarters and you can tell us every-thing that happened."

They set out into the castle. Danny was seriously wondering if the lord mayor was still alive. Surely this was something he'd want to sit in on. He didn't especially care one way or the other, but clearly something was wrong with the way Rosenbar was run.

Lyra shifted over beside him. "Going after that drake on your own was incredibly dangerous."

"Yes, but given the alternatives it seemed like the best choice. Had our positions been reversed, what would you have done?"

"The same thing, but that doesn't make it wise. You should've seen the kings' faces when I told them what you did. I haven't been so amused in about three centuries."

"Glad I could help."

They reached the vice mayor's quarters, an elaborate suite complete with a huge dining room. Levett rang for a servant and everyone asked for whatever the kitchen was preparing. They settled around the table with Levett at the head.

"We're all eager to hear what happened," Levett said. "Why don't you begin, Hero?"

Danny obliged, leaving out the bit about the ring and the ethersword. Assuming he survived the final battle, no one needed to know about his wish and if he died, it would be a pleasant surprise. As for the backup sword, it was weaker than the hero's sword, so there was no need to use it.

When he finished Lyra shook her head. "I can't imagine how much time it took them to capture and subdue a fire drake. None of the other demon kings tried anything remotely that ambitious. I wonder how long our enemy has been preparing."

"Do you think that's why it took so long for this cycle to begin?" Dufour asked.

Lyra shot him a glare, though it held little real heat. It seemed like a reflexive move rather than a genuine one. "Very possible. From the kingdoms' point of view, the cycle doesn't start until we spot the demon king's forces approaching. For all we know, the current demon king was summoned forty years ago and has spent all this time gathering the largest army we've ever faced."

"What a cheerful thought," Balen muttered.

"He did more than that," Danny said. "We've confirmed two churches and I'm sure they aren't the only ones."

"No doubt," Lyra said. "We certainly never saw them during our past battles in Fell Forest. Anyway, the kings have agreed to a change of plan. Half the combined army will pull back and begin hunting down the raiding forces. We are to head directly to Demon King Castle. If there's an army waiting for us, we pull back. If not, we attack and end it."

Sounded like a reasonable plan to Danny. He'd be glad to have this over with sooner rather than later.

# CHAPTER 27

T he trip from Rosenbar to what everyone had thought would be the front line took nearly two weeks. Since Lyra wanted to get there as quickly as possible, they rode in a mostly straight line, camping out in the open. Not the safest way to travel by any means, but by some miracle, nothing attacked them on their journey. On the downside, they did find two villages burned to the ground without a body to be seen. When Danny mentioned it, Lyra said they were likely either devoured by monsters like the others or animated as thralls or undead.

Talk about terrible possibilities.

It was dusk when the army camp appeared ahead of them, sprawled over a space about half the size of Rosenbar. They'd set up tents, dug trenches, and built a barrier of sharpened wooden stakes. Other than the tents, Danny couldn't see much point to it all. The stakes wouldn't make a demon break stride. Maybe it was to keep the local wildlife out.

The camp was buzzing with activity. Wagons were being loaded with supplies as soldiers scrambled here and there.

Beside him Lyra let out a little growl. "It's been ten days and ninety percent of the army is still here. They should be on their way back to their respective kingdoms by now. What's the holdup?"

This was one question Danny could answer with confidence. "It's the army. Everything takes forever. Apparently it's the same on every planet in the universe. Does it change our plans?"

"No. We sleep here tonight then make for the castle once the sun is fully risen. We should arrive around noon or a little after three days later."

"Does the sun weaken users of corruption?" Danny asked. "Also, three days in Fell Forest is going to be an issue."

"No, but it does make the forest a bit brighter, so we'll be better able to see any potential threats. It's a tiny thing, but every little bit helps. As for the time we'll need to spend in the forest, that's unavoidable. Most of us can use holy magic to some degree. We'll have to manage. All the other groups did. How are you doing? You seem calmer than I expected."

"I've made peace with what's coming. It has to happen so getting worked up will only make me tense and exhausted. Not exactly the best state to face the most dangerous person in the world."

"Whatever happens," Lyra said. "You'll be remembered forever."

Danny kept his expression sober but inside he was smiling. He almost hoped he died fighting the demon king just so he could see the look on Lyra's face when he came back.

They reached the outer pickets and Lyra urged her mount

to the front. Danny was happy to let her take the lead again. He might be the hero, but he hadn't met all the important people in this world, unlike her. The only way it would work was if he wore the armor all the time, a prospect he didn't find appealing. On the other hand, it seemed like everyone knew Lyra. How many pointy-eared women with glowing eyes could there be?

The guards on duty didn't even have a chance to speak before Lyra said, "Lyra Shael to see General Benoit. He's expecting us."

"Yes, Lady Shael." The right-hand guard stammered a bit as he spoke. "We received word of your pending arrival and were told to send you and the hero directly to the command tent. It's in the center of camp."

The guards scrambled to drag a portable gate out of the way. As soon as they did, Lyra guided her horse through without a word.

Danny smiled at the guards. "Thanks, fellas. Stay safe out here."

They didn't seem quite sure how to respond and soon Danny was out of earshot. He remembered plenty of thankless nights on guard duty. At least Danny hadn't had to worry about demons. Just insurgents, grenades, RPGs, and snipers. Those were the days.

The soldiers outside were all too busy running around to pay them any attention and soon they reached the center of camp and the huge tent standing there. A long hitching post provided a convenient place to tie up their mounts. Lyra didn't bother announcing herself. Instead, she just brushed the tent flap aside and walked in. Balen glanced at him as if he was surprised.

Danny shrugged. "She's like this with pretty much

everyone save the king. I don't think she means anything by it, it's just her way."

He hurried to follow her and the others came along behind him.

The inside of the tent wasn't what Danny was expecting. There were no gaudy decorations or luxurious furniture. There were tables covered with maps, a few hard chairs, and a cot. Other flaps hid the remaining rooms, so that might be where the fancy stuff was.

A short, round man in a red-and-gold tunic and black trousers stood at the central map table. His bald head shined in the warm light. He gave off a distinct Napoleon vibe which convinced Danny that he had to be the head man.

When Lyra reached him he glared up at her. She glared right back down at him. Perhaps they knew each other.

"Lady Shael, this plan of His Majesty's is most irregular. Dividing our forces is madness. If I only have half my soldiers and the demon army attacks, we'll be overrun in hours."

"Is that why you're slow-walking the redeployment, General?" Lyra asked.

"I hoped I could convince you that this is folly and you'd send a message to His Majesty explaining that we shouldn't change plans."

"I'm not certain there is a demon army," Lyra said. "As far as we can tell, the enemy portaled their forces past you to wreak havoc on the peasants. Multiple villages have been burned and many hundreds slain. And the slower you are to redeploy your troops, the more innocent people will die. Think about that as you delay."

The general had the good grace to look sheepish. "I've

read all the histories, Lady Shael. The war never goes like this."

"I lived the histories and you're right, but it seems this demon king is more creative than the last six. We'll be staying in your camp for the night and heading into the forest in the morning. If there's an army waiting, we'll be back quickly. If not, hopefully Daniel can end this cycle."

General Benoit looked over at Danny and his companions, clearly not sure which of them was the hero.

"I'll do my best tomorrow, sir," Danny said. "We're counting on you to help save as many innocent lives as possible."

The general drew himself up to his rather unimposing height. "You may depend on me, Hero."

Danny offered a polite bow. "Could we get something to eat? It was a long trip with nothing but trail rations. I want to be at full strength for tomorrow."

"Of course. I arranged a tent for you. Nothing fancy, I'm afraid, but we have to make do in the field."

"Isn't that the truth." Danny stepped closer and held out his hand. "Pleasure to make your acquaintance, sir."

Benoit gave his hand an enthusiastic shake. "Likewise, Hero, likewise. This will be a moment I tell my grandchildren about. May Adonael bring you victory. And rest assured that our forces will be on their way in three more days at most."

"I'm confident you'll do your utmost for the good of the Five Kingdoms." Danny extracted his hand from Benoit's grasp. "Is there anything we can do to hasten the process?"

"No, no, it's all under control. I'll have someone show you to your tent. Food will be brought as soon as it's ready."

"Excellent, thank you."

A few minutes later the group was following a nervous boy who looked younger than Danny's host body. Their guide brought them to a canvas wall tent that brought to mind something out of a western.

"This is yours, my lord," the youth said. "I'll bring your meals shortly."

With that he hurried away.

They stepped through the flap and Dufour conjured a light. There were eight cots lining the walls and nothing else of note. Better than sleeping on the ground but not by a lot, assuming fantasy cots weren't more comfortable than the ones from his world.

"You handled the general well," Lyra said. "You almost sounded like a courtier."

"Thank my new memories for that. I just did what they said and added a bit of my own. I've dealt with high-ranking officers before. They tend to like a bit of flattery. I'm supposed to be a celebrity in this world, I figured I might as well play that up. If it gets the troops moving faster, then I'm glad to do so."

"It shouldn't be necessary," Lyra said. "Orders were sent and they should be swiftly obeyed."

Danny shrugged. There was nothing he could do about that. He settled on the nearest cot and found it reasonably comfortable. Hopefully he could get a full night's sleep before setting out tomorrow. He doubted any of them would sleep well in Fell Forest.

# CHAPTER 28

When Danny led the way into Fell Forest, he did so in full armor and with the hero's sword at his side ready to go. That had been two and a half days ago. They were close to the castle now; he could feel it despite the protection afforded by his armor.

This part of the forest felt completely different from the previous areas he'd visited. Despite the bright sunlight, it seemed dimmer and colder. Even the sound of their footsteps was muted. The corruption in the air was so thick it should've been visible to everyone.

He glanced at Lyra and found her expression as tense as he'd ever seen it. She'd barely spoken during the morning meeting with General Benoit before they set out. Given her annoyance with the army's commander that might have been just as well. The meeting hadn't amounted to much beyond a quick chat to let him know they were leaving. The general wished them luck and renewed his promise to hurry the redeployment. She hadn't relaxed since.

Balen groaned, staggered a few steps, and vomited noisily behind a tree. Danny was once again reminded how lucky he was to have mithril armor. It purified the ambient corruption, leaving him free of side effects.

The swordsman finished, wiped his mouth, and turned to face them. "How much worse is it going to get?"

"Very much," Lyra said. "We're still several miles from the castle."

"Then let me cast another protective spell," Eve said. "The demons will sense Daniel's mithril anyway."

"I didn't ask you not to cast a second blessing out of fear we'd be detected, but rather because of the toll it will take on you to maintain it for hours," Lyra said. "If you're confident in your stamina, then please, the protection will be most welcome."

"If it will help," Danny said. "Feel free not to include me in the spell. The corruption isn't affecting me at all."

"One less person will definitely help." Eve closed her eyes and a golden glow appeared around her hands. The glow spread from her to the others, including Lyra. The tension on their faces vanished, only to reappear on Eve's.

"You okay?" Danny asked.

"As long as I don't have to fight." Eve grimaced. "Or walk too fast."

That didn't sound okay to Danny, but the longer they delayed the worse it would get, so he stayed quiet and they set out again. Another couple miles passed without any sign of demons.

"Am I the only one that thinks this is weird?" Danny asked.

"No," Lyra said. "Last time we had to kill over a hundred

demons before we got within sight of the castle and that was after the demon king's army had marched against ours. This emptiness worries me more than if we were fighting for our lives."

Danny was afraid she was going to say that. Still, there was nothing they could do besides press forward. So they did.

An hour later the forest opened up, revealing a huge, black, stone castle. There was nothing elegant about the construction. It was blocky and ugly, with winged demons serving as gargoyles on the walls and towers.

He looked closer. Maybe they were real demons. Danny couldn't tell from this distance.

No outer wall surrounded the keep. In front of the entrance stood six figures in black armor. They held massive black greatswords engraved with bloodred runes. None of them made any move to advance. They just stood there waiting.

"So do we go down and say hi or what?" Danny asked.

Lyra shook her head, looking totally flummoxed. "I don't see any other option. There really isn't an army. I doubted it, but I can't argue with my own eyes."

"Six of them plus the demon king and six of us plus the hero," Dufour said. "That can't be a coincidence."

Danny glanced at Eve, who was panting, her face twisted into a pained grimace. "Whatever's going on, we can't screw around trying to figure it out. You guys will only grow weaker and weaker as the corruption eats away your strength. Let's just do this."

He marched forward and the others fell in behind him. When they were about fifteen paces away one of the demon warriors stepped forward and bowed to them. "Welcome, Hero. Our mistress offers you safe passage to the central chamber where a one-on-one battle to decide the fate of the world will be held. We will be sure to entertain your companions in your absence."

Danny glanced at Lyra. "What do you think?"

"I think you need to go and defeat the demon king as quickly as possible. Once that's done, the corruption will lessen, allowing us to fight on even terms. We'll be counting on you."

"Right. Good luck, everyone." Turning back to the demon warrior he said, "I accept your terms."

"Very well." The warrior held out his hand. Danny tensed. A crimson orb appeared above his palm. "Follow this guide."

Hand on the hilt of his sword, Danny walked between the rows of armored knights. If ever there was a moment for them to attack, this was it. None of them flinched, then he was past. The keep door opened and he strode through behind his gently bobbing guide. Empty black halls exuded an oppressive aura. There were no demons, no servants, no nothing including decorations. Just blank black stone everywhere you looked. His guide provided the only light. Even his boots thunking on the floor sounded muted.

"Dracula's going to want this place back at some point," Danny muttered.

The hall ended up being a straight shot to the central chamber. A heavy black door opened at his approach. Inside he found a large open space with a black disk in the middle that looked exactly like the ones in the churches only about three times bigger around. A single figure stood in front of it. She, at least Danny assumed it was a she based on the hips, wore black mail armor and a helmet that included a full mask. A slim sword hung at her waist.

"Welcome, Hero." Her voice was warm and rich, full of promises he didn't want to think too hard about.

Danny silently activated a psychic protection spell. "Hi. I'm not sure exactly what's going on, but you've managed to thoroughly confuse everyone. What's the point if our fight is going to settle everything anyways?"

"I serve a demon lord. Death, destruction, and chaos are their own rewards." She came closer, her steps a sensual strut. Danny tightened his grip on the hero's sword. "Be at ease. I wish to speak with you a bit before we attempt to kill each other. Why did you not take my servant up on her offer to join me? We could rule the world together."

"Mostly it's the whole 'murdering innocents' thing. I'm not a fan of that. Now, as much as I'm enjoying our chat, my companions are busy fighting your bodyguards. And I can't help them until I deal with you."

"Why do you care? These people are strangers to you, or near enough. I felt it when you were summoned. It's been, what, six weeks, two months at most? You can't possibly have formed much of a strong attachment to them already. You're a victim, brought here against your will. I'm offering you a chance for revenge against those who wronged you."

Danny tightened his grip on his sword. "Yeah, like I said, killing innocent people isn't my thing. The villagers your ogres ate didn't summon me. They certainly didn't do anything worthy of getting devoured."

The demon king—or was it queen?—sighed. "So be it. Though I'll warn you, even if you defeat me, the world's problems won't end."

"One of them will. The rest I can worry about tomorrow."

He kicked the ground hard, cracking the stone as he pushed off. Despite his speed, somehow the demon queen got her black sword out and made the parry.

And then the battle was on.

Danny pushed his physical enhancements to the very edge of what his body could take. He feared if he held back in the slightest that black sword would find a gap in his armor.

The clash of mithril against black iron filled the central chamber.

It sounded like machinegun fire the blows came so fast.

A missed slash crashed into the wall, sending chunks of stone flying.

Danny's heart raced and he feared something might explode.

Sweat dripped into his eyes, blurring his vision.

He blinked it away and sent a blast of lightning at the demon queen.

She batted it away with contemptuous ease. He hadn't thought magic would work, not with her aura of corruption, but better to check.

The demon queen leapt back over the portal, forcing Danny to sprint around it.

As he ran, she launched spears of darkness at him.

Danny slashed them apart without slowing.

This could go on forever. He needed to end it before his body gave out on him. Just because he had another life in his back pocket didn't mean he was eager to try it out.

No, the only way he could win was to take a foolish risk. Perhaps that was what got the other heroes killed. He didn't know but he was about to find out.

Danny tightened his grip on the hero's sword and pulled

every drop of ether into his body that he could. And then he kept going until it felt like he was going to explode.

Then he charged.

The ground exploded under his feet with each stride. His bones cracked and his muscles tore as they were pushed beyond human endurance. Blood leaked from the corners of his eyes as he honed his vision. Every sense was sharpened.

He saw where he needed to strike. There was a tiny gap in the demon queen's armor. Two of the links hadn't been forged perfectly. Danny never would've seen it without pushing his vision to this degree.

She swung her sword to block his thrust, but her movements were too slow.

The hero's sword smashed through the flaw, cut through her chest, and burst from her back.

The black sword clattered from her hand. Danny pulled back his enhancements and fought to stay upright. His whole body hurt. It felt like he'd gone twelve rounds with a baseball bat.

"Well struck," the demon queen said.

Despite having a sword through her chest, she spoke with no sign of pain. She reached up and removed her helmet, revealing a beautiful, pale face. Dark hair spilled out around her.

"Thanks, I guess."

"You think you've won," she said. "But you're mistaken. All my death will accomplish is hastening the world's destruction. So thank you for that."

Danny shook his head. This chick was nuts. Though he knew that already since she worshipped a demon lord.

"I'll worry about that when I have to. I'd like to say that

it's been fun, but it really hasn't." He ripped the sword free and drew back to cut her head off.

Before he could, a pillar of dark magic exploded out of her. When it faded, she was gone.

Did he win? Did she escape? Danny didn't know what the hell happened. He'd have to ask Lyra. But first, a quick nap. He hit the ground and stared up at the ceiling before closing his eyes.

# CHAPTER 29

Lyra found herself locked in battle with two of the black knights. Despite their size, their greatswords darted around like rapiers. She turned a slash aside and danced out of the way of a thrust that would've skewered her. The sounds of the other battles clattered away at the very edge of her awareness. She would've liked to help the other companions, but it was taking all she had just to survive. None save the first demon king had ever pushed her this hard in a fight. Granted, it was two on one, but still, she should've been able to handle two demon warriors.

She leapt back and hurled a stream of fire that they both ignored. With the local ether so corrupted, her magic was all but useless. All she could count on was physical enhancement and a magical aura for her sword.

Her opponents charged in together.

One went high and the other low.

Lyra leapt between their swords and rolled to her feet. That had been too close.

They didn't give her time to celebrate her survival.

The duo bore in again, forcing her to fight defensively. The heavy blows from their weapons made her sword hand tingle. She was getting nowhere. At least there hadn't been any shouts of pain which meant the others were holding their own. Lyra didn't want to think about what might happen if she had to fight three or more on one.

She slipped on a loose rock and for an instant was wide open. The demon warriors attacked, but more slowly than before, giving her time to recover.

Out of the corner of her eye, she spotted Eve looking her way, hands raised. The priestess must have done something to slow them. Lyra had never thought much of Adonael's choice for high priestess, but Eve was holding her own when it mattered.

A dagger came flying in. It struck the left-side warrior in the helmet and exploded, knocking him ten yards back.

Not wanting to waste Aline's effort, Lyra charged the remaining warrior. Her sword became a blur as she slashed and thrust. Her frustration grew as strike after strike was either turned aside or skipped off the demon's breastplate. This thing had to have a weakness. She'd killed more demons than she could count. No way were these two invincible. She was missing something.

The second demon recovered and the pair went back on offense. Once again Lyra found herself on the very edge of death.

Fighting with total defense, she watched their moves, looking for patterns. She'd been so focused on winning quickly that she'd skipped this part. An amateur mistake. Had she seen one of the heroes make it, Lyra would've given them an earful.

After a few seconds a pattern did emerge. The demons

took turns being more offensive. One always hung back a fraction to cover any openings its partner might leave. That was good to know, but didn't give her any hints on how she might defeat them.

Snarling her annoyance, Lyra resigned herself to just trying to survive until something happened to change the odds.

The battle raged on with no change in the balance. Lyra held her own, but couldn't find an opening to strike. And then a dark pillar exploded out of the castle. As soon as it did, the demons slowed.

Daniel did it. Nothing save the death of the demon king could explain the dark pillar. She'd seen six others like it after all.

Pushing her advantage, she darted in and sliced the throat of one demon, nearly taking its head off. A moment later she stabbed the second one through the armpit and it collapsed and started to dissolve as well. Her path to the castle was clear. She needed to reach Daniel quickly. The battle would've taken a huge toll on his body.

She strengthened her protective barrier and shouted, "I'm going after Daniel! Don't follow me! It's too dangerous for you."

And with that she sprinted for the castle.

The front entrance was open and unguarded. Lyra didn't slow as she raced through the dark halls. The layout was exactly the same. She often wondered why none of the demon kings ever changed anything, but in the end it didn't matter.

She reached the central chamber and found Daniel lying on the ground a few feet from the portal. Lyra grimaced as the pain increased. Standing this close to the portal, even diminished as it was, took a toll on her. She had to get Daniel out of here before she grew too weak.

Steeling herself, she crossed the chamber.

With every step she feared her body might burst into flames. She was well familiar with the pain and her divine blood offered some protection. The other companions would've been killed in seconds, assuming they somehow made it this deep into the castle.

When she finally stood over Daniel she looked down into his closed helmet and found his bright blue eyes staring back at her.

"What's a nice elf like you doing in a place like this?" he asked.

The words came out slurred and barely intelligible. He'd no doubt taken some head trauma.

Lyra grabbed him and forced him to his feet. "Let's get out of here."

"Good idea. Did you know the demon king was a woman? She tried to recruit me again. Have to give her credit for determination."

"I didn't know that." Lyra dragged him toward the exit. "Though it may explain the vastly different tactics she used. You had no trouble killing her?"

"I had great trouble killing her. She was fast and strong. It took everything I had, but I finally ran her through the chest. That didn't stop her from talking. Before I could cut her head off, that pillar of darkness consumed her. That's the last thing I remember before seeing you."

They passed through the doors to the central chamber, which slammed shut behind them, cutting off enough of the corruption that she merely felt sick.

"Let's rest a minute." She guided him to a little stone ledge running along the hall that led to the exit and he sat. "That pillar consumes every demon king. I saw it all six previous times. Take your helmet off and let me check your head. From the sound of your voice I think she must have hit it."

Daniel undid the chin strap and slid his helmet off. "She hit everything. Even the drake wasn't this difficult of a fight. But I survived and she didn't. Can't ask for more than that."

"Turn your head as far to the right as you can. I want to check the back of your skull." Lyra moved to the left and slipped a dirk silently out of its sheath where he couldn't see it.

He did as she asked. "How are the others?"

"Fine. They're all fine. You did amazing, Daniel. The entire world owes you a great debt."

She slammed the dirk through the base of his skull. Daniel's body twitched a few times then slumped over. Lyra pulled the blade out, cleaned it, and put it away. A little fire magic sealed the tiny hole. His long hair hid the scar perfectly.

With a deep sigh, she shifted some power to physical enhancement and picked up his body. She moved like a golem, keeping her emotions tightly under control. She would need to vent them at some point, but not yet, not until she finished her task.

When she left the castle, the outer gates slammed shut just as the inner doors had. The companions had finished their battles and, as she told Daniel, they were all alive, though far from unscathed.

Eve spotted her first and came running over. "No, no, no! What happened?"

"Daniel defeated the demon king only to die in the end himself." Lyra gave a sad shake of her head that was only partially feigned. "I don't know if it's the universe's way of maintaining the balance or something else, but I'm weary of burying the heroes I train. Let's go."

Paul and Balen came closer. "Would you like us to carry him?"

They were both covered in shallow wounds and one of Balen's arms hung limp at his side.

"No, I'm fine. I'd like to do this final thing for him. Once we leave Fell Forest behind, Eve can purify his body and we'll dig a proper grave. We owe him that."

"We owe him far more than that." Eve sniffed and wiped her eyes. "But it seems a new statue behind the cathedral will have to be enough."

# EPILOGUE

T he trip back to the capital was a long and gloomy one for Lyra and the others. They'd made a brief stop to let General Benoit know that there wasn't an army waiting to attack him then continued on their way. Very little conversation was had as everyone appeared lost in their own thoughts. That suited Lyra fine as she had no desire to talk with any of them.

As soon as they passed through the gate, Lyra bid them farewell.

"Wait!" Eve said. "Where are you going? Shouldn't we have a wake for Daniel? Raise a glass to his memory or something?"

Lyra shook her head. "That isn't the elvish way. Daniel's gone and we honor him in our hearts. If you wish to do something for him, by all means, do so. Right now, King Richard needs to know what happened. Then I'm going to see my granddaughters."

She nudged her horse into motion and quickly left her human companions behind. The idea of raising a toast to the man she'd killed turned her stomach. It took all she had not to let her feelings show. None of them could ever know what she did. While she doubted the companions would care one way or the other, Eve was another matter. The kind-hearted priestess would raise no end of hell should she learn the truth.

The castle guards waved her in and Lyra dismounted in front of the keep. Having no desire to speak with anyone, Lyra used her magic to locate the king. He was in the war room. Not surprising given the current situation.

She hurried through the halls, ignoring both curious servants and guards as she passed. The war room door was closed and she nearly barged in. Instead she knocked and said, "It's Lyra."

"Come in."

She pushed the door open and found Richard on his own in front of the map. There were a great deal more black pins in than the last time she was here.

"Is it done?" Richard asked.

She closed the door and cast a sealing spell. "The demon king is dead and so is the hero. We buried him in a pretty little glade about half a day from Fell Forest. The armor and sword are back in my pocket dimension. You know, I'm not sure Daniel would've asked for anything other than a bit of peace and quiet and enough to live on."

"We couldn't risk it. The first hero nearly bankrupted the kingdom. Never again. After he saved everyone, we wouldn't have been able to deny him anything. And we need those resources to rebuild." Richard waved at the table. "Look at this. There have been attacks everywhere. Thousands slaughtered. And that might end up being a blessing in disguise since a third of the harvest was also destroyed.

Those deaths might be the only thing that lets the rest of the people avoid starvation. This might be the worst loss we faced in any cycle and there are still Adonael knows how many monsters and demons still roaming the countryside."

"I understand, but that doesn't mean I have to like it. I've obeyed your orders as I swore to. Nothing more."

Richard nodded. "And your people will continue to enjoy the Crown's protection, as I and my ancestors promised. Take some time to recover. We'll have a ceremony honoring the hero in a week or so. I'll announce his tragic death defending the kingdom tomorrow."

He turned back to the map and Lyra happily accepted the casual dismissal. The trip back to the mansion felt especially long today. Knowing she'd have to tell her granddaughters their new friend was dead no doubt had something to do with it.

○

Danny woke in the pitch black with an oppressive weight crushing him. He couldn't breathe or move. Panic rushed through him. He lashed out with an unrefined blast of ether. The explosion cleared whatever had been trying to crush him. He sat up and brushed something off his face. When he opened his eyes he found his hand covered with dirt. In fact he was sitting in a hole about six feet deep.

Then it all came back to him. Lyra oh-so-kindly helping him out of the central chamber. Lyra acting worried about him as he asked about the battle. Let me check the back of your head, she said. Danny had been so out of it, he hadn't considered not doing as she said.

Then a sharp pain and the lights went out.

Didn't take a genius to know what happened. It also didn't take a genius to figure out what happened to the other heroes. Did any of them actually die at the hands of the demon king? He couldn't know, but had his doubts after what happened to him. He also wondered if the demon queen had known his fate and tried to save him. That was another thing he'd never know.

What he couldn't figure out was why his wish had brought him back to life buried alive. That wasn't safe. And it didn't feel like he was still in Fell Forest, which meant more than a day had passed. Maybe even three or four. How had his wish been this badly misinterpreted? But then again, Merrok had warned him the magic was tricky.

Well, whatever, he was alive again and that was the important thing.

He got slowly to his feet. Despite being buried alive he felt fine. Well, in his companions' defense, he'd technically been buried while dead. He touched the finger where his ring should've been. He had supplies and the ethersword in storage. He'd need both if he wanted to survive.

Fortunately, Danny knew where to find his ring. Maybe Lyra would refuse to give it back. He smacked his fist into his palm. In fact, he rather hoped she did.

He meant to get revenge, his and all the other heroes'.

# AUTHOR NOTE

Hello everyone,

I hope you enjoyed the beginning of Danny's adventure. This are only going to get more exciting in book two, The Birth of Ronin, so I hope you'll join me when it arrives.

If you don't want to miss any of my new releases, deals, general news about the Etherverse, you can signup for my newsletter on my website.

www.jamesewisher.com

Until next time, thanks for reading,

James E. Wisher

# ALSO BY JAMES E. WISHER

Summoned to Another Words and Forced to Fight The
Demon King

The Summoned Hero

The Birth of Ronin

The Fate of The Five Kingdoms

The Plague Lands

Elfhome

The 72 Demons

The Blood of Solomon

A Friend in Need

The Demon Masks

Hunt For The Devil Man

The Immortal Apprentice Trilogy

The War With Audin (Prequel Novella)

The Hunt For Revenge

The Army of Darkness

The Apprentice Reborn

The Soul Bound Saga

An Unwelcome Journey

Darkness in Tiber

Depths of Betrayal

The Black Iron Empire

Overmage

The Divine Key Trilogy

Shadow Magic

For The Greater Good

The Divine Key Awakens

The Portal Wars Saga

The Hidden Tower

The Great Northern War

The Portal Thieves

The Master of Magic

The Chamber of Eternity

The Heart of Alchemy

The Sanguine Scroll

Shadow of The Dragons

The Dragonspire Chronicles

The Black Egg

The Mysterious Coin

The Dragons' Graveyard

The Slave War

The Sunken Tower

The Dragon Empress

The Dragonspire Chronicles Omnibus Vol. 1

The Dragonspire Chronicles Omnibus Vol. 2

The Complete Dragonspire Chronicles Omnibus

The Complete Aegis of Merlin Omnibus

Other Fantasy Novels:
The Squire
Death and Honor Omnibus

The Rogue Star Series:
Children of Darkness
Children of the Void
Children of Junk
Rogue Star Omnibus Vol. 1
Children of the Black Ship
Children of The End

# ABOUT THE AUTHOR

James E. Wisher is a writer of science fiction and Fantasy novels. He's been writing since high school and reading everything he could get his hands on for as long as he can remember.

www.ingramcontent.com/pod-product-compliance
Lightning Source LLC
Chambersburg PA
CBHW022005010726
47494CB00003B/904